Wild THING

Wild THING

Emma Barnes

Illustrated by Jamie Littler

SCHOLASTIC

First published in the UK in 2014 by Scholastic Children's Books
An imprint of Scholastic Ltd
Euston House, 24 Eversholt Street
London, NW1 1DB, UK
Registered office: Westfield Road, Southam, Warwickshire, CV47 0RA
SCHOLASTIC and associated logos are trademarks and/
or registered trademarks of Scholastic Inc.

ISBN 978 1407 13795 7

A CIP catalogue record for this book is
available from the British Library.

Printed and bound by CPI Group (UK) Ltd, Croydon, CR0 4YY
Papers used by Scholastic Children's Books are made
from wood grown in sustainable forests.

1 3 5 7 9 10 8 6 4 2

www.scholastic.co.uk/zone

For Abby, the Wild and Wonderful

Wild THING

She's a demon child
She's not meek and mild
She's wild!
Oh yeah. . .

She can bite
Oh yeah and she can fight!
She'll give you a fright!
Oh yeah!

She's wild, wild, wild!
Yeah!
Oh she's wild, wild, wild. . .

I have a problem. Her name is Wild Thing. (At least that's what I call her.)

Unfortunately, Wild Thing is my sister.

That means it is really difficult to get rid of her.

Not that I haven't tried.

PET FOR SALE

Would make wonderful guard dog – watch out!
Nasty bite.
Bad temper. Sharp teeth. Loud bark.
Hates baths.
Yowls in the night.
Eats marshmallows, sardines and ice cream.

My dad laughed like a drain when he read this.

"That's our Josephine," he said. (Josephine is Wild Thing's real name.) "But you know, Kate, you can't sell her."

"Why not?" I asked. "*I* don't want her, that's for sure."

"Yes," said Dad. "But nobody else will, either. Wild Things don't make good pets."

He had a point. "Hmm," I said. I thought about doing another sign.

SISTER FOR SALE –
going cheap!

Do not miss this opportunity to acquire a darling little girl!

Name: Josephine.

Age: five years old.

No fleas.

All her own teeth.

Loves to sing and dance!

Answers when called - well, sometimes.

I was struggling. It is hard to think of nice things to say about Wild Thing.

Maybe I was going about it all wrong. Maybe I should try and exchange her instead. I would have *loved* a real pet – a snuffly rabbit or the scruffiest little pup. Instead, I was stuck with Wild Thing!

At that moment she came into the room. And my heart dropped.

She was crawling (although she can walk perfectly well). She was carrying the microphone from her karaoke set in her mouth, like a dog carrying a stick. And she was wearing purple knickers, and nothing else. Except for jam. Jam on her face, jam on her tummy and jam in her hair. There was even jam on her purple knickers.

Nobody would ever buy her, I thought. They probably wouldn't take her if *we* paid *them*. Even if they did, they'd return her within the hour.

Wild Thing dropped the microphone on the floor. She sat back on her heels. "I've lost the guitar," she announced. "From my Monkey Magic band."

Dad didn't look too concerned by this news.

"Oh well," he said. "I can't look for it now."

Wild Thing's Monkey Magic Band are four toy plastic monkeys the size of toothpicks. Two of them play guitar, one of them has a plastic drum kit and the last one is the singer. Dad's friend Wes gave them to her.

"But I need it!" squeaked Wild Thing.

"It's tiny," said Dad. "It would be like looking for a needle in a haystack. Or a guitar pick in our living room."(Dad is a guitarist.)

"I know where it is," said Wild Thing.

"Then how can you have lost it?" I asked.

"'Cos it's stuck. That's why."

Wild Thing pointed. For a moment we were

6

puzzled. She was pointing at herself. And sort of pulling her head back and squinting. Suddenly we understood.

"Oh no," groaned Dad, slapping his hand against his head. "It *can't* be true! Don't tell me the daft child – she hasn't – she *can't* have. . ."

But she had. Yup, you guessed it.

SHE'D STUCK IT UP HER NOSE.

I began to giggle. I couldn't help it. Then Dad and I got down on our knees and peered up into Wild Thing's nose.

Yeuch! It was dark up there, and we couldn't see much. (Not even snot, I'm glad to say.) So I got my torch, and we shone it upward and there it was. Wedged in her left nostril. A tiny, plastic guitar.

"Josephine!" Dad grumbled. "What did you do that for?"

He didn't sound surprised, though. Because it is exactly the kind of thing Wild Thing DOES do.

"*I* didn't do it," said Wild Thing. "Punky Monkey did it."

"Who's Punky Monkey?"

"He's the singer. Look. He's over there." Wild Thing pointed under the kitchen table. We couldn't see anybody.

Wild Thing is always imagining things. She hangs out with imaginary animals and princesses and pop stars all the time. My teacher last year, Mr Brice, was always saying that imagination is a wonderful thing. I don't agree.

I mean, I bet Mr Brice never had to take *his* little sister to the hospital because an imaginary monkey stuck a plastic guitar up her nose.

He wouldn't think imagination was so wonderful then!

Not that we took Wild Thing to the hospital straight away. First we tried to get the guitar out ourselves. I shone the torch while Dad tried to grab the guitar using a pair of tweezers.

"Is it a guitar I see before me," said Dad thoughtfully. "Or is it *not*? *Not* – *snot* – geddit?" He chuckled away at his own joke.

"That's *snot* funny," I said, grinning.

"Keep still," Dad told Wild Thing. But Wild Thing wouldn't. She wriggled and squirmed. She wriggled so much that Dad jabbed her accidentally with the tweezers. And then she screamed.

Boy, did she SCREAM.

When she stopped screaming, she started shrieking.

"HELLLLLP!" she shrieked. "HELP, HELP!"

"Who do you think's going to help?" I asked. "Punky Monkey?"

"Bother!" said Dad, peering up Wild Thing's nose. "I think it's gone further in."

"Maybe it will go all the way up her nose and get stuck in her brain," I said.

Dad gave me a reproachful look. Wild Thing started yelling even louder than before.

"I DON'T WANT A GUITAR IN MY BRAIN!"

"It won't go into your brain, you juggins," said Dad. He groaned. "We're going to have to take her to the hospital. . ."

"Not *again*!" I said.

". . .And I'm meant to be teaching this afternoon."

Dad teaches guitar as well as playing it. His students come to our house for lessons. And he doesn't like to let them down.

But there was nothing else for it. Dad went to call his student and I tried to get Wild Thing dressed. It wasn't easy. She refused point-blank to put on her jeans. In the end I had to let her wear her Disco Diva costume instead.

Her Disco Diva costume is a pair of gold trousers and a red top with *DISCO DIVA!* written across the front in gold sequins.

She loves to dance, does Wild Thing. And to sing. Unfortunately her dancing looks like the Wild Things in that picture book, *Where the Wild Things Are*, when they are doing their Wild Rumpus. And her singing sounds like the cats next door when they're fighting. And then she starts leaping about doing air guitar – and she looks like a mad monkey, not a little girl at all.

I guess that's why we call her Wild Thing. Because that's what she is!

Wild Thing's shoes had all gone missing – at least I couldn't find a matching pair – so she wore a luminous orange wellington boot on one foot, and a plastic beach shoe on the other. She looked very odd, I can tell you. Even odder than usual.

At last we set off for the hospital. Only just

as we were loading Wild Thing into the car, our neighbour Mrs Crabbe came rushing up and said what was all that SCREAMING and SCREECHING? It sounded like somebody was being murdered – so she had phoned the police, just in case!

Dad, who had been apologizing for the noise, looked alarmed.

"What did you do that for?" he said. "Why didn't you just call us or come round?"

"I *did* call you," snapped Mrs Crabbe, "and I *did* come round. I knocked and banged and kicked at that door for AGES and nobody answered."

(It was true. We found the dents in the door afterwards to prove it. Wild Thing had been making so much noise that we just hadn't heard.)

"I was so, so worried," went on Mrs Crabbe reproachfully. "I mean, I know you musicians are peculiar . . . but screaming and banging at two o'clock in the afternoon—"

"Dad's not peculiar!" I protested, but at that moment a police car pulled up. It had flashing lights and a siren was blaring, and two policemen (actually one of them was a policewoman) leapt out of the car as if they thought there really *was* a murderer on the loose.

I was impressed. I mean, Wild Thing has done lots of terrible things in her time, but nobody's ever called the police before.

Wild Thing was excited too. "Arrest her!" she yelled at the top of her voice, pointing at Mrs Crabbe. "She's a dangerous criminal!"

"I am not!" Mrs Crabbe went all red, and her neck wobbled like a turkey's. I told Wild Thing to be quiet while Dad explained to the police what had happened.

Luckily, the police had a good sense of humour. And one of them (he was called PC Blunt) actually peered up Wild Thing's nose to take a look for himself.

"By gum," he said, "there really is something stuck up there." And then he said, "Kids, eh?" and that even his youngest, who's a right little tearaway, had never done anything *that* bad before.

"Mind you, he did once stick a pencil down his sister's ear."

"Please don't give her any ideas!" I said, hurriedly.

"Well, we'd better get to the hospital," said Dad. "Sorry to waste your time, Officer."

"Not to worry," said PC Blunt. He looked up and down our street. "You know, there've been a few break-ins round here recently. I hope you locked the front door before you left?"

"Of course we did," said Dad, a bit impatiently.

"Because locking up is the sort of thing it's easy to forget when you're rushing your little girl to the hospital. And you wouldn't like to come back and find you'd been burgled."

Dad said he distinctly remembered turning the key in the lock. But I ran back to check, and he hadn't.

So then Dad went and locked up.

Finally we left for the hospital!

All the way, Wild Thing was singing at the top of her voice.

"She's not meek and mild
She's a demon child
She's WILD!
Oh yeah. . .

She can bite
Oh yeah and she can fight!
She'll give you a fright!
Oh yeah!

Wild, wild, wild!
Wild, wild, wild!"

Dad actually wrote this song. He used to perform it with a band called Monkey Magic. (Dad played guitar. His mate Wes was the lead singer. He still is, actually. I think that's why Wes gave Wild Thing the toy monkey band – he thought it was a good joke.)

I hate this song. Perhaps it's something to do with the fact that it's Wild Thing's favourite. She sings it *all the time*, in her horrible, screechy voice. She's convinced that it's all about her – even though Dad says that it's not.

"Stop it, Wild Thing!" I yelled.

But of course she took no notice.

Now you can see why I want to sell her!

One thing I've noticed about hospitals (from our regular visits with Wild Thing) is that there's a lot of waiting around. I suppose if Wild Thing managed to saw her own arm off, they'd probably be a bit quicker to see her. But with the kinds of things she does we just have to sit and wait.

And wait.

Like the time she glued a sardine tin to her head. We were there most of the night. I actually wished that I'd brought my pyjamas!

This time the coffee machine had run out. That made Dad grumpy.

The snack counter was closed. That made *me* grumpy.

And Wild Thing kept running round and

round the waiting room asking if anybody wanted to look up her nose.

That got on everyone's nerves.

Everyone except for a boy about Wild Thing's age. He was drinking a carton of juice, while his mum was busy with a whinging baby.

"*I'd* like to look," he said.

"OK then," said Wild Thing.

I nudged Dad. He shrugged. "Just pretend she's not ours," he whispered, and started checking messages on his phone.

The little boy peered up Wild Thing's nose.

"Can you see it?" Wild Thing asked. "Can you see the guitar? It's stuck! Only the doctor can get it out!"

"*I'll* get it out," said the boy.

Wild Thing was surprised. "How will you?"

"With this." He waved the plastic straw from his orange juice carton. "I'll stick this up your nose and *suck* it out."

My jaw dropped. I waited to hear what Wild Thing would say. She thought about it for a long time. "No," she said at last. "It might have germs." (As if Wild Thing ever usually worried about germs!) "And what if you sucked out my brains?"

The boy didn't give up. "I'll give you a toffee," he said, waving one in front of her.

"OK," said Wild Thing. Obviously she'd rather have a toffee than brains!

"*Dad!*" I muttered, jabbing him with my elbow.

"Josephine, come here now," said Dad.

"No!" shrieked Wild Thing. "Want toffee!"

Luckily, before she could launch into a full-scale tantrum, the nurse called out her name. We dragged her into the treatment room and Dr Whitely became the fifth person that day to have the pleasure of peering up my sister's nose!

His face looked very solemn as he examined her. Suddenly I felt nervous. Would Wild Thing be OK? Perhaps the guitar had gone too deep! Perhaps they really would have to cut into her brain!

Wild Thing didn't seem nervous – but she *was* in a very bad mood. She had really wanted that toffee! Besides, I don't think she likes doctors. She's met too many of them. When this one got out his tweezers, she started to scream.

"No, no, no!" she screeched.

Then she tried to run away. We shut the door and barred her way. *Then* she tried to bite the doctor. In the end, me and Dad had to hold her down.

"Got it!" yelled Dr Whitely, waving the little guitar.

"Whoo!" said Dad. He wiped his forehead. Then he thanked the doctor and apologized for Wild Thing's behaviour. "She's – er – had some bad experiences with doctors, you see."

"I know," said Dr Whitely cheerfully. "I was the only one who would see her!" He winked at me and added, "Only joking!"(though I'm not sure he was). He handed Dad the little plastic guitar, then said, "Hey, don't I know you from somewhere?"

"I don't think so."

"I'm sure I do. . . I know, you used to play guitar with Monkey Magic!"

"Yes I did, that's right," said Dad.

"I saw you do a gig once, years ago. They're quite big now, aren't they? How come you left the band?"

"A long story," said Dad.

"A shame you left before they made the big time. . ."

Dad wasn't really paying attention. He was edging out of the door after Wild Thing. She had run back into the waiting room as soon as we'd let go of her.

". . .So what do you do now?"

By this time we could hear raised voices.

"I still play guitar," said Dad, quickly. "Thanks for your help."

We ran into the waiting room. The little boy was lying on his back on the floor. Wild Thing was sitting on top of his chest like a contestant in a wrestling match. She was waving a bag

over her head triumphantly, while a bunch of
nurses and patients were staring at her, open-
mouthed.

"Toffee!" she yelled. "Toffee! Tofffeeee! ALL
MINE!"

4

"They must be sick of the sight of her at that hospital," said Gran, after I had finished telling her the story.

We were sitting in the garden. Dad was putting kebabs on to the barbecue. Wild Thing was jumping about, making a hideous din with her castanets. She was down at the overgrown end of the garden (nobody in our house has much time for gardening) and every now and then her head would pop out of the leaves like an orang-utan out of the jungle.

Gran had just got back from holiday in Spain. Just about the first thing she had done after unpacking was to come round to our house. I was really pleased to see her. (Though I did wish she hadn't brought Wild Thing the castanets.)

"Still – all's well that end's well," said Gran, settling back in her deckchair. She was looking all tanned and smiley after her holiday.

"It didn't end well!" I said. "Do you know the worst thing of all?"

"Tell me," said Gran.

"The nurse gave her a badge. Guess what it says?"

"What?"

"It says I WAS A BRAVE GIRL IN HOSPITAL. And she wasn't. She was *awful*."

Wild Thing must have heard. She dropped the castanets and came charging towards us at top speed.

"I *am* a brave girl," said Wild Thing, sticking out her chest. "It says so here!" She pointed at the badge. She had been wearing it every day since she went to hospital.

"It says so, but it's a big fat lie!"

"Not a lie!" shouted Wild Thing. She stormed off.

"Don't worry, Kate," said Gran, patting my

24

arm. "You'll be back at school tomorrow. Then she'll be out of your hair."

"That's what I'm worried about," I said. "This year *she's* coming to school too!"

Wild Thing was really looking forward to Big School, as she called it. But every time I thought about it, I felt queasy. I liked school *without* Wild Thing.

At school I can just be me. I mean, I guess some people know that my dad is a bit different from other dads. They've seen him often enough, with his jeans and his long hair and stubble and his guitar case slung over his back.

They've seen Wild Thing, too, sitting on the back of Dad's bike. You can't really miss her – especially if she's yelling the Wild Thing song! But they just laugh. They even think she's sweet. Hardly any of them know how awful she is.

Of course, my best friend Bonnie does. She lives on my street, and knows only too well how wild Wild Thing can be. One time Wild Thing rode Dad's guitar case like a surfboard *down* the stairs and crashed into Bonnie, who was on her way up! Luckily Bonnie doesn't hold that against me. And she's always good fun, even if she's bossy sometimes.

But when Wild Thing gets to school (unless she has a complete character change), *everyone* will know about her.

I think Gran understood how I was feeling. "Remember, she'll be in the Little Ones," Gran pointed out. "They don't even have the same lunchtime. They've even got their own playground. You probably won't notice she's there."

I cheered up. Perhaps Gran was right.

Gran gave me a mint from her handbag. She called Wild Thing over and gave her a mint too.

"Not that you deserve one," she added. "Sticking a guitar up your hooter!"

"Not my *hooter*," said Wild Thing. "My nose." And she stuck her finger up a nostril to show

Gran exactly what she meant.

"Get your finger out of there!" barked Gran. "Your hooter *is* your nose, silly!"

"How can it be?"

"It's just another word for it. Like your bottom is your behind. And they should have given you a good smack on yours," Gran muttered.

(Gran believes in smacking, or so she says. Though Dad says she's all talk. She's certainly never smacked us.)

Unfortunately, Wild Thing has always been very interested in bottoms. So she loves any chance to talk about them.

"Bottom!" she yelled delightedly. "Gran said *bottom*! Behind means bottom! And bottom means bum."

And she started dancing about, wiggling her bottom at us and shouting, "BEHIND! BOTTOM! BUM!" at the top of her voice.

"Quiet, Wild Thing!"

"Gran said bottom!"

"No, she didn't."

"Yes, she did." Wild Thing grinned. "A butt is a bottom. You've got a big butt!" She pointed at me. "And Gran's got a wrinkly one!"

Then she danced off across the garden, shouting, "BUTT! BEHIND! BOTTOM! BUM!" at the top of her voice. She almost crashed into a tree.

Gran had stopped being all relaxed from her holiday. She was making noises like an angry dragon. I don't suppose anybody likes to be told they have a wrinkly butt. Wild Thing was lucky she was out of *her* reach!

"Shut up," I shouted after her.

My sister ignored me. "I'm doing the Bottom Boogie!" she called.

She waggled her bum at us.

Still waggling, she sang her Wild Thing song.

"She can fight

Oh yeah and she can bite!

She'll give you a fright—"

And when she got to "fright", she pulled down her jeans and mooned us!

It sure was a nasty *fright*, the sight of Wild Thing's bare bum sticking out at me.

"Right!" I yelled. I'd had just about enough of my sister. I leapt up. "I'm gonna get you!" I told her. "And when I do – I'm going to BITE THAT BUM!"

(It must have been the word "bite" in the song that gave me the idea.)

I ran at her. Wild Thing screeched with fright. She managed to get her jeans back up. Then she set off across the lawn.

But I had a head start. And she is only five.

"Hah!" I shouted, leaping towards her. "I'm a wolf and you're a rabbit!" I'd forgotten to be angry. Actually, I was enjoying myself. It was great to have my sister on the run!

Wild Thing dodged round the bushes. But she wasn't going to dodge me for long!

"Gotcha!"

I grabbed her. She squeaked but I held on.

And then I bit her on the bum.

I really did.

Not hard. I mean, it wasn't a big bite. It didn't draw blood. Or even graze her jeans. It was just a little *nip*, really. Just to show her.

But Wild Thing acted like I had sunk my teeth right in.

"Owwwwww! You *bit* me! You BIT me! With your teeth!"

She carried on so much that I began to feel bad. I had only meant it for a joke. Maybe I'd bitten harder than I'd thought.

"Oh, oh, oh!" shrieked Wild Thing. Her face was bright red.

"Look," I began, "I didn't mean—"

"You *bit* me! You really did!"

"Now listen—"

"DO IT AGAIN!"

"What?" I said.

Wild Thing jumped up and down in front of me. "Go on!" she begged. "Please, Kate! Try and bite my bum again!"

Would you believe it? That sister of mine thought I had just invented the best game in the world. And she couldn't wait to play again.

I could hear Dad and Gran laughing in the background. I shook my head. Then I couldn't help it. I started to chuckle. The next moment, we were all laughing so hard it felt like we'd never stop.

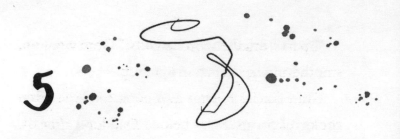

5

All the time we were eating our barbecued sausages and vegetable kebabs, Wild Thing kept going on and on *and on* at me to try and bite her bottom. "Go on!" she yelled. "Bite my bum!"

"I think you've started something, Kate," said Dad.

"I know I have," I groaned. I could see I was going to spend weeks with Wild Thing nagging at me to play Bite the Bottom.

"How are the kebabs?" asked Dad. He smiled nonchalantly. "Home-made, you know." Dad fancies himself as a cook. He's always watching the celebrity chef shows on the television.

"Not bad," said Gran.

Dad preened.

"Apart from the scorched bits," Gran went on, smothering her kebab in ketchup.

Gran fancies herself as a cook too. She often cooks tea for us. She's helped Dad look after us, ever since Mum died when Wild Thing was only tiny.

I like Gran a lot. But I still miss Mum sometimes.

"You did buy all the girls' school things, didn't you?" Gran said now, munching on her kebab. "You know, like I reminded you before I went to Spain." Gran is very practical. Unlike Dad.

Dad immediately looked guilty. "Yes," he said. "I mean – no. I mean – what school things?"

Gran tutted. "*School things,*" she said very slowly. "Socks. Tights. Cardigans. PE kit. Water bottles. Lunch boxes—"

"Actually I haven't," said Dad. "But, after all, school doesn't start till Tuesday."

We all stared at him.

"Tomorrow *is* Tuesday!" said Gran.

I added, "You doofus!"

"Oh, ham sandwiches!" said Dad. Only he didn't say ham sandwiches. He said a bad word that I'm not supposed to use, and I'm not going to write it down here.

Gran tutted. She doesn't like it when people use bad words.

"They don't really *need* those things, though, do they?" said Dad hopefully. "I mean, who needs socks? Or lunch boxes?"

"They need them," said Gran firmly. And that's why Dad ended up taking me and Wild Thing to Big Supermarket that very evening.

We call it Big Supermarket because it's big. Actually it's enormous. Gran won't go there because she says it makes her feel giddy and she's scared of getting lost. Big Supermarket stays open all night. And it sells lot and lots of things.

We found tights and socks and gym shoes for me and Wild Thing. We found lunch boxes too. Though Wild Thing didn't choose the pink one with the picture of kittens that most five-year-old girls would choose.

Oh no. Wild Thing chose the one with a scary monster on the front.

Then Dad and Wild Thing went to look at water bottles. I could hear them arguing because they couldn't find one that matched her lunch box – *"I don't like pink, I like monsters"* – but then I spotted Bonnie. She was standing near the toilet-roll section with her big brother, Zach.

Zach is nice. He's a whole year older than us. Actually, I'm quite shy of him, if you want to know the truth.

"Hey," I said, going up, "did your mum forget to buy *your* school things too?"

"Oh no," said Bonnie. "We bought *our* stuff *weeks* ago."

She didn't *mean* to sound snooty (at least I don't *think* she meant to sound snooty) but she *did* sound snooty, all the same.

"Oh," I said.

Bonnie and Zach's mum is *very* organized.

She's not the sort of parent who would ever forget what day school was starting. Not like Dad.

"We're here because there's a special offer on dog food," said Zach.

Bonnie's family have two enormous dogs, Sugar and Sweet, who aren't sugary and aren't sweet. They have huge teeth and red eyes and slathering jaws, and remind me of Fluffy from *Harry Potter*.

Once when I was sleeping over at Bonnie's, and needed the toilet in the middle of the night, I went on to the landing and Sugar and Sweet were standing there. They just *looked* at me, but I was so scared that I was frozen to the spot. Luckily Bonnie's mum came out and found me, or I'd have been standing there all night.

That was a few years ago, though. I'm not scared of them any more. Well. Not most of the time.

They both eat an awful lot of dog food.

"Mum never misses a special offer," said Bonnie. "If she gets a text alert, then she's straight down here."

"I don't think my dad even notices the special offers," I admitted.

"Well, I wish Mum was a bit more chilled, like your dad," said Zach. (He really *is* nice.) "And I'd love to have a dad who's a rock guitarist."

"Would you?" I asked curiously. To be honest, I often wish Dad was something more normal, like a teacher or a dentist, and had teacher or dentist friends, instead of musician friends who come round the house at strange hours and make lots of noise "jamming". A dentist would turn up at school wearing a shirt and tie, and he wouldn't ever be late because he was writing a new song and forgot the time!

(Not that I don't like music. I do. I'm learning the saxophone and Dad's taught me some guitar. But not a lot of people know this, as I'm not a great big show-off – unlike some people in our family.)

"Oh yeah, I'd love it!" Zach went on. "Especially if he played with Monkey Magic!"

I remembered what Dr Whitely had said. "They're quite big now, aren't they?" I asked casually.

"They're huge!" said Zach. "I love their songs! We're learning them in guitar club at school—"

But I didn't hear any more because at that moment—

"OWWW!" I shrieked.

I had suddenly felt a sharp pain in my posterior. And posterior, in case you don't know, is another word for your butt, behind, bottom or plain old bum!

It felt as if somebody had just bitten me there.

Somebody *had*. Wild Thing!

She was getting her revenge. I should have known she wouldn't forget the Bottom Biting Game!

Bonnie and Zach were both laughing (Zach was trying not to, because he is so nice, but he couldn't help snorts of laughter bursting out).

I couldn't believe that Wild Thing had done something so terrible in public, in a supermarket and *right in front of my friends*.

"I'm gonna get you, Wild Thing!" I said.

Wild Thing raced off. I went hurtling after her.

I almost crashed into Bonnie's mum and her trolley full of dog food. Then in the next aisle – Bread Products – I nearly knocked over a pretty woman with black hair. In fact, I trod on her toe.

"Ouch!" she said, glaring at me.

"Sorry!" I called over my shoulder, as I dashed onwards towards Breakfast Cereals. And it was in Breakfast Cereals that I finally caught up with Wild Thing.

"Gotcha!" I yelled, putting on speed.

The floor was slippery. We were both going much too fast.

CRASH!

We ploughed straight into a shelf of breakfast cereal.

PLINK! PLUNK! PLONK!

Boxes of breakfast cereal came raining down on to our heads.

I was planning to bite Wild Thing's bottom – or maybe give her a good kick there instead – but all those cereal packets took the wind out of me. I just sat there gasping. I pictured the news headlines.

"CRUSHED TO DEATH BY AN AVALANCHE OF MALTY POPS!"

"My favourites!" shrieked Wild Thing, hugging a packet to her chest. "I want to buy them *all*."

Several shop staff were heading towards us. Judging by the expressions on their faces, I had a feeling we might have to!

6

Wild Thing is what Gran calls an Early Bird.

She's what I call a pain in the neck.

(Or maybe I should make that bottom.)

Every single morning of the summer holidays I'd been woken by the horrible sound of Wild Thing screeching in my ear, followed by her bouncing around my room like a ping-pong ball, then sitting on my head. Tuesday morning was no exception.

"Get out," I moaned, covering my ears. "Go back to bed."

"But it's school today, SCHOOL TODAY!" yodelled Wild Thing, jumping up and down on my bed like she was competing in the World Trampolining Championship.

I groaned. She was right. You can't sleep in on

a school day. I pushed back the covers and slid my feet out of my lovely, warm bed.

I looked at my clock.

It was five thirty. FIVE THIRTY A.M.!

"It's practically the middle of the night!" I protested. "We don't have to be up until seven!"

"But—" said Wild Thing.

"No buts!" And I shoved her out of my room and slammed the door.

"But I'm too excited to sleep," said Wild Thing, sticking her head round my door as I climbed back into bed.

"I don't care! Do some colouring. Anything! Just leave me alone!"

I lay there, fuming. I was so mad it took me ages to get back to sleep. When I woke again the house was strangely peaceful. I lay there thinking how nice it was.

Then I looked at my clock.

I flung off my duvet and shot out of bed and into Wild Thing's bedroom like a cannonball.

"Wild Thing! It's *eight o'clock*! Why didn't you wake me?"

Wild Thing was lying on her front, colouring. She looked up. "You told me not to wake you," she said primly. "So I didn't."

"But – but – but. . ."

I gave up and rushed to find Dad. I wondered how he had slept through his alarm clock. I soon found out. He had never even gone to bed. He was fast asleep on the sofa downstairs.

"GET UP!" I bellowed. "We're late!"

"What has she done now?" yelled Dad, leaping off the sofa with his hair on end and his eyes staring. (He must have been dreaming about Wild Thing.)

"It's what she *hasn't* done," I told him. "She hasn't woken us. And you – why aren't you in bed?"

Dad explained he had been watching a great late-night TV show about blues guitar. "I, er . . . I guess I dozed off."

I tutted.

"You sound just like Gran," said Dad accusingly.

I pursed my mouth up, the way Gran does when she doesn't approve, and waggled my finger at him. We both chuckled. Then we raced to make breakfast and fill lunch boxes. Wild Thing strolled in waving her picture. "I've drawn ten sunflowers," she told us.

"I don't care if you've drawn the Eiffel Tower," I said. "Get dressed now!"

So she did. She got dressed really quickly too. She was back in the kitchen in five minutes.

"I'm ready!"

"Good," I said. I was filling the water bottles at the sink. I turned round and – "What are you wearing!" I shrieked.

Wild Thing was wearing her Rock Chick outfit: shiny gold boots, purple leggings and a T-shirt which says *Rock Chick*. She also had her wig on. It's black and bushy and Dad always says it makes her look like Ozzy Osbourne. *I* think it makes her look like a wicked witch.

Wild Thing looked puzzled. "Well, I'm wearing
my Rock Chick T-shirt and my leggings and—"

"I can see that!"

"Then why did you ask me?"

"Because you can't wear that to school,
chicken head!" It came out as a real growl. I

sounded like Sugar and Sweet when somebody comes too near their bone.

"Yes I can," said Wild Thing. "I can wear anything. I need to express myself!" She began to sing her Wild Thing song, but I grabbed her and hauled her upstairs and shoved her into her school uniform.

At last we were ready. Dad was riding his bike as usual. He had his guitar case slung over his back, and Wild Thing sitting at the back in her special seat. They rode down the street, and Wild Thing waved at passers-by. Sometimes she called out: "I'm going to school!"

I followed on my own bike. We passed Zach and Bonnie in the Walking Bus, and then lots of people climbing out of their parents' cars. They all stared like anything.

But we made it on time! My very first day at school with Wild Thing!

7

My class has a new teacher. She is called Miss Deng and she has just joined our school.

Here are some interesting facts about Miss Deng:

1) Her family comes from China, and she has shiny, straight black hair and sparkly eyes that are shaped a bit like almonds. I think she's very pretty. Definitely a lot nicer to look at than Mr Brice last year, who had a nose like a potato with hairs growing out of the nostrils!

2) She's musical. She's going to take orchestra *and* direct the school musical and decide who gets which part.

3) She's strict. And a bit scary. When she says, "Quiet now," her eyes flash and everyone stops talking. Even the back table.

4) One more thing. Remember the lady I trod on in Big Supermarket? When I was chasing Wild Thing through the Bread Products aisle? Well, that was Miss Deng. I even saw her rubbing her foot at one point – probably trying to ease the bruise.

For a while I told myself that she hadn't recognized me. After all, I'd been past her in an instant. But then, when we were writing in our writing books about "What I Did in the Summer Holidays", she kept giving me funny looks. Her eyes narrowed. Her mouth made a hard, thin line.

She recognized me all right.

Was she thinking:

That's the sweet child who was running after her high-spirited little sister in the supermarket?

Oh no. She was thinking:

That's the little hooligan who almost knocked me over. I'm going to keep an eye on her!

So much for my chances of being in the school musical! What a terrible start to the new term!

At lunchtime, Bonnie couldn't stop talking about Miss Deng, and how wonderful she was, and how she, Bonnie, was going to get her hair done in exactly the same style. (As Bonnie's hair is red and curly and Miss Deng's is black and pencil straight, I couldn't see how this would work, but I didn't say so.)

"I just wish she didn't hate me," I said. "She blames me for what happened in the supermarket, I know she does, and now she'll never give me a part in the school musical." I sniffed sadly, then took another bite of cheese sandwich.

Bonnie sipped orange juice with a thoughtful expression. "Look at it this way – she'll soon find out about Wild Thing, and how dreadful she is. She's bound to! And when she does, she won't blame you any more. She'll probably feel sorry for you, having a sister like that!"

I know Bonnie *meant* to be comforting. But I didn't find her comforting at all. After all, if Miss Deng found out how awful Wild Thing was, so would everyone else. And I didn't want that!

But then Bonnie gave me half a chocolate-cherry cupcake her mum had made. That really did make me feel better!

Gran came to meet us from school. And would you believe it? She had brought Wild Thing's old pushchair with her.

"But she's *five!*" I protested. "Nobody goes in a pushchair when they're five!"

"Yes, but it will have been a long day for her," Gran said. "Besides, I thought we might go round by the park."

Just then Wild Thing appeared. She immediately plonked herself down in the pushchair. She only just fitted. In fact, I'm surprised the pushchair didn't break.

"Thank goodness!" Wild Thing heaved an enormous sigh. "This has been a Very Tiring Day!"

"*Tiring!*" I said. "In the Little Ones? Colouring in? Listening to stories? Finger painting?"

"Do up your belt, Josephine," Gran told her. "I don't want you to fall out."

"*Fall out?*" I said. "She can't fall out. She's *wedged.*"

Wild Thing just shrugged.

"Do up your belt," said Gran, more sharply.

Wild Thing ignored her.

"*Josephine,*" said Gran. It was her dangerous voice. The one that means *you'd-better-do-it-now-or-you'll-catch-it.*

"I'm doing the STUPID belt," Wild Thing said.

Only she didn't say *stupid*. She used a different word. A bad word. One of those bad words that Children Are Not Supposed To Say.

Some of the parents nearby looked round and tutted. Some of the children went "*Oooooh!*"

Gran went on the attack.

"*Josephine!* I hope you didn't say what I thought I heard you say!"

So then Wild Thing said it again. Louder.

"I'M JUST DOING THE STUPID BELT!" (Only not stupid but the bad word.)

She was so loud I think this time the whole playground heard.

Gran went scarlet. She really hates swearing. Some of Dad's friends swear a lot – though Dad says they don't mean any harm – but Gran always says there's no excuse. She was about to let rip at Wild Thing, but before she could say anything, Miss Randolph appeared.

Miss Randolph is Wild Thing's new teacher. She likes to wear flowery clothes and jangly bracelets, and she's always smiling.

"Do you think I could have a little word with you?" she said to Gran. "It's about Josephine."

"Of course," said Gran. But she didn't look happy.

It's never a good sign when somebody wants a

"little word" about Wild Thing. You can bet your life it's not going to be:

"Josephine has been particularly kind and helpful today"

or

"Josephine is already a valued member of our school community"

or

"Josephine did such wonderful work we are planning to give her a prize."

"We have a few little problems with Josephine," said Miss Randolph. *Here we go*, I thought. "You see, for one thing she won't sit down."

"Won't sit down?" echoed Gran blankly. She looked at Wild Thing. "What's all this then?"

"Don't want to sit down," said Wild Thing. "In playgroup I didn't sit down."

"No, but we do need the children to sit down in school," said Miss Randolph. She spoke in the soft, cooing voice she uses with all the Little Ones. As if they are sweet little bunny rabbits, instead of terrible terrors like

Wild Thing. "They have to sit down to listen to their teacher. And to hear the lovely stories. And to drink their delicious milk. I'm sure you want to do all these lovely things, don't you, Josephine?"

"No," said Wild Thing.

"We'll have a talk with her," Gran told Miss Randolph.

"That's not all," said Miss Randolph. "When everyone else is singing, she does this." She demonstrated.

"Oh, that's playing air guitar," I said. "She loves to play air guitar."

"Well, I've never met a five-year-old who plays air guitar . . . not while all the others are singing 'If You're Happy and You Know It Clap Your Hands'. And not while yelling *Wild Thing!* at the top of her voice so that everyone can hear her, all the way down the corridor." Miss Randolph's face went all crumply. "She said it was boring!"

"It *is* boring," said Wild Thing. "I don't want

to sit in a circle and clap! I don't want to listen to *her* –" she pointed at Miss Randolph "– play the boring old piano!"

"But Wild Thing," I told her, "you're at school now. You have to behave. Even when it's boring. Not that Miss Randolph is boring," I added quickly. "Even when she does play piano. I mean – especially when she plays piano. I mean. . ."

I decided to shut up.

"One more thing," said Miss Randolph.

She held something up. It was pink and *hairy*.

We stared at it.

"She hasn't cut off the guinea pig's tail, has she?" asked Gran in a shocked voice.

"Guinea pigs don't have tails," I said.

Miss Randolph said, "It's her own hair. She cut it off with the scissors from the Craft Corner." Her voice was a lot less sweet and cooing than usual.

"But her hair isn't pink," I pointed out. "It's brown."

"I painted it pink," said Wild Thing. "I wanted a pink stripe. But *she* said I shouldn't have. So then I cut it off."

And now that I looked I could see the bald patch where my sister had cut out a big chunk of her own hair. I was amazed I hadn't noticed it before.

"*She* didn't like that either," added Wild Thing, pointing at Miss Randolph accusingly, as if it were all her teacher's fault for being so difficult to please.

Gran exploded. "But why did you paint a pink stripe?"

"'Cos I'm Wild Thing!" yelled Wild Thing. "Yeah, yeah, yeah, man!"

She tried to leap up, maybe to do her Wild Thing dance, or maybe to try and bite Miss Randolph's bottom for all I know. But she was so tightly-wedged that the pushchair came with her. The whole thing tipped over. "Help!" squawked Wild Thing from under the pushchair.

Miss Randolph and Gran began shouting and fussing with the pushchair. Lots of other parents and kids rushed over to "help" – which meant shouting and fussing too. Everyone else was staring and pointing.

I felt so embarrassed that I wished it was me under that pushchair. At least then I wouldn't see all those people staring at us!

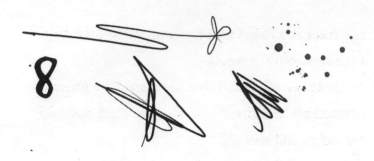

8

Gran was babysitting us that evening because Dad was going out to a gig and wouldn't be back till late. It was a band he really liked, and he was excited about hearing them. He was rushing around getting ready, and didn't have a lot of time to listen to what we were saying about Wild Thing and school.

"Well, it sounds like it all went off quite well, really," he said as he searched for his wallet.

"Quite well!" I repeated in disbelief. "Are you joking?" I counted off on my fingers. "One – she wouldn't sit. Two – she wouldn't sing. Three – she told her teacher her piano-playing was boring. And four – she cut out a big chunk of her own hair!"

"At least it was her *own* hair," Dad pointed out. "She could have cut off another child's hair. Or her teacher's hair. Or something *worse* than hair. Like somebody's nose."

"Eek!" I said. But at that moment Dad's friend honked his horn from outside, and Dad grabbed his jacket and was off.

Gran made us tea. She made her Famous Welsh Rarebit. I don't know why it is called that. It's not Welsh and it's not rare – not in our house, anyway; we eat it all the time. And it's not famous either – not outside our house.

It's just what everyone else calls cheese on toast.

Still, it's yummy, so we don't care.

Afterwards we had Gran's Famous Jam Roll with Custard, and after that we felt VERY FULL INDEED. Like we always do after what Dad calls "one of your gran's light suppers".

"I feel so full I could burst," said Wild Thing, sticking out her tum and banging on it like a bongo drum.

"How about some fruit to finish off?" said Gran.

"Don't like fruit," said Wild Thing. "I like marshmallows, sardines and ice cream."

"Not together, I hope," said Gran.

Wild Thing thought this was really funny. She laughed and laughed, like it was the best joke ever. She was laughing so much she fell off her chair and rolled around on the floor– which is not a good idea, if your kitchen floor is cleaned as rarely as our dad cleans ours. She ended up with an old oven chip stuck in her hair.

Then Wild Thing wanted to make marsh-mallows, sardines and ice cream, there and then. She reckoned it might be a wonderful new invention. Gran made her go and have a bath instead.

I stayed to chat with Gran.

"Do you know that Monkey Magic are really big now?" I asked her.

"Are they?" asked Gran. She didn't sound that interested. Gran is not into rock music – she prefers the kind of music they play at her tango classes.

"Yes," I said. "Zach said so and so did the doctor at the hospital. And when I looked on their website it said they're going to be touring America soon!"

Gran sniffed. "I wouldn't fancy rattling around America in an old van!"

"They're probably travelling in jets and limousines!"

"I wouldn't fancy rattling around America in jets and limousines, then."

"Well, I would," I said. "I think it would be really interesting and glamorous. If I went, I'd wear sunglasses all the time, like a celebrity, and I'd go to lots of parties, and eat all my meals from room service."

"You'd always be bumping into things if you wore sunglasses. And hotel food is never anything special, in my opinion," said Gran. She gave me a curious look. "Anyway, I can imagine Josephine enjoying those things, Kate, but not you. You don't like to be the centre of attention."

I could feel myself blushing. "Sometimes I do – in my head."

"What do you mean?"

"Well – like in my *head* I'd like to be in the school musical. But in real life, I'm too scared!"

It was true. I could imagine myself dancing across the stage, or standing in the spotlight singing a big number. But when it came to it – I just knew I'd freeze, and the words wouldn't come out. And everyone would be staring at me, the way they did at that terrible Christmas carol concert years ago at school. I was supposed to sing solo – and I still remembered that horrible feeling of my heart thudding and my stomach churning, and when I finally did get the words out, they came in a tiny mouse squeak!

Gran brushed my cheek with her hand. "You and Wild Thing – you're a funny pair. She needs to show off less, and you could do with showing off more!"

She went back to stacking the plates. I leaned against the kitchen counter. "Why *did* Dad leave Monkey Magic, anyway?"

"Well, he could hardly look after you and

Josephine if he was going off on tour for weeks on end, or staying out all night, every night, now could he?"

"Oh," I said.

"He wouldn't have enjoyed all that rock star nonsense anyway," said Gran firmly.

I went upstairs slowly. In a way, it made me feel really big and important that Dad had given up being a rock star for me and Wild Thing. But I wondered how Dad felt about it. He did love playing guitar. Gran said Dad didn't mind – but I wasn't so sure. Maybe Dad was missing out.

On the landing I bumped into Wild Thing, who was skipping out of the bathroom, butt naked, waving her towel around like she was a bullfighter.

"Wild Thing," I said. "Did *you* know that Dad might have been famous if it hadn't been for us?"

"What d'you mean?" asked Wild Thing.

"I mean he could have been a Big Rock Star. And rich. And on the telly. He could have worn sunglasses all the time, and drunk champagne for breakfast, and. . ." (my imagination was in overdrive now) ". . .gone everywhere by helicopter or in a purple limousine."

Wild Thing thought about this, with her head on one side.

"*I* think. . ." she said.

"Yes?"

"I think that *I'd* like to be a Big Rock Star. And when I am, Kate, *you* can drive my limousine."

I stared at her in horror. It was about the worst idea I'd ever heard in my whole life.

Wild Thing a Big Rock Star! Yuck!

That night I had a dream. I was lying next to a swimming pool, wearing sunglasses and a diamond necklace and sipping a milkshake with a cherry on top. Then a crocodile stuck its head out of the water. It crept out of the pool and slithered towards me. Suddenly, I woke up.

Something was climbing into my bed.

Something cold.

For a horrible moment I thought it really was the crocodile. Then I realized it was Wild Thing – which was almost as bad.

"Go away," I snarled.

Wild Thing was next to me. Her feet were cold as icicles. She was breathing in my ear, and it tickled.

"I *can't*," she whispered.

"Why not?"

"'Cos there's a monster!"

I groaned. "I've told you before, *there are no monsters under your bed.*"

"Not under the bed," said Wild Thing. "Downstairs."

I groaned again. Wild Thing and her overactive imagination!

"There's only one monster in this house," I told her, "and it's in this room right next to me!"

Wild Thing squeaked with alarm.

"It's YOU!" I said. "*You're* the monster. Go back to your room this minute!"

But she wouldn't.

"I want to stay with you!" she said.

I looked at my watch. It was almost two o'clock. *Two o'clock in the morning!* Gran would have gone home by now. Dad must be fast asleep.

I was too tired to argue. "All right, you can stay. But *go to sleep!*"

Only Wild Thing wouldn't. She wriggled. She squirmed. She nagged.

"Tell me a story! *Pleeeease*, Kate!"

So in the end, I did. I quite enjoyed it, actually.

The story was about a Monster. The Monster lived in a cave.

For breakfast, the Monster ate a little girl with toast.

For lunch, he ate a little girl with ketchup.

For supper, he ate a little girl with cheese.

And for his snacks, he ate little girl chopped morsels.

And guess what – all the little girls looked just like Wild Thing!

I thought it was a great story. I wondered why teachers never gave us things like that to write at school, instead of boring old *What I Did in the Summer Holidays*.

Wild Thing didn't enjoy it, though. She didn't go to sleep either. "That monster's going to get us!" she kept saying.

"Go and wake Daddy then," I said. "'Cos I've had enough!"

Wild Thing slid out of bed. A few minutes later she was back.

"The monster's got Daddy!"

"WHAT?"

"It's true! He's not in bed."

"He's probably just gone to the toilet," I said. But I thought I'd better go look for him anyway. Maybe he could get my sister back into her own bed, where she was supposed to be.

But when I arrived at Dad's bedroom, I got a nasty shock. His bed *was* empty. The covers were all strewn around too . . . just as if a monster had dragged him from his bed! And there was nobody in the bathroom either.

There was a fluttery feeling in my stomach. I didn't believe in monsters. *Did I?*

I crept down the stairs and peered into the hall. Gran's coat and bag weren't on their hook. So she had definitely gone home. But where was Dad?

The door to the living room was a little bit

open. Through the gap, I could see something . . .
strange. Something . . . *big*. Something . . .
well . . . it was hard to be sure from that distance,
but something that looked . . . *scary*.

I could hear a strange noise too. A kind of . . .
growly noise.

I began to feel very peculiar – as if somebody
had poured cold water down my spine.

Suddenly there was a sound behind me. I
almost jumped out of my skin.

It was Wild Thing. She came charging along
the landing, waving the battle mace from her
Knights in Armour set.

"What are you doing?" I hissed.

"Out of my way!" said Wild Thing, and she
charged down the stairs.

9

"Wait!"

I ran at Wild Thing and tried to grab her. But she dodged me and was in the hall before I could stop her.

I raced behind, but she was too quick. She bounded into the living room and the next moment I heard terrible noises – shouts and thumps!

I flung myself after her.

There really *was* a monster! It was black and purple and writhing around on the sofa like a giant worm, while Wild Thing clonked it with her battle mace.

"Take that!" she yelled. "And that!"

"Ow!" bawled the monster.

Suddenly I noticed a head poking out one

end. And that's when I realized that it wasn't a giant worm. It was Dad's friend Wes – the lead singer from Dad's old band, Monkey Magic. He was in one of the purple and black sleeping bags we keep in the cupboard under the stairs.

"Wait! That's not a monster!" I yelled, trying to haul her off.

"What's going on?" asked Dad, sticking his

head round the door. As soon as he saw what was happening he raced over to help me.

We both held tight on to Wild Thing – who was acting just like her name, spitting and scratching – while Wes crawled out of his sleeping bag, groaning and rubbing all the sore bits where Wild Thing had bashed him.

"Your kids are wild, man," Wes moaned at Dad. "One minute I'm just resting my eyes – having a lie-down – the next moment Psycho Girl here is bashing me over the head with a club!"

"It's a battle mace," I said helpfully.

"Well, whatever it is, it's not good for the head!"

It turned out Wes and Dad had met up at the gig, and Wes had come back afterwards to hang out and also to hear the latest songs Dad had written. It had got too late to go home, so Dad had told him he could sleep on our sofa. When Dad had gone off to find an extra blanket, Wes had climbed into his sleeping bag and fallen asleep.

He had woken up to find Wild Thing clubbing him over the head!

"A nasty shock, man," Wes kept saying, rubbing his head.

"Well, you looked like a monster," said Wild Thing, not sounding at all sorry. "And you sounded like one too."

"I did not! Did I, Katie?"

"You did a bit," I said. "You were snoring."

Wes must be a champion snorer – after all, Wild Thing had heard it all the way from her bedroom!

Not that Wes would admit to this.

"I am *not* a snorer," he kept insisting. "I never, ever snore!"

"You do so!" said Wild Thing.

I had to agree with her. "Those are the loudest snores I've ever heard in my life! It sounded like somebody drilling the road!"

"Or an elephant harrumphing," Wild Thing said.

I snorted with laughter. But then I did my

best to look serious as I gave Dad and Wes a right telling-off for being up so late. After all, Gran wasn't there, so it was my job!

"Do you realize it's two o'clock in the morning? It's ridiculous. And on a *school night* too!"

"Yeah – sorry about that," said Wes. "Down to me. I wanted to hear your dad's new song."

"Well, you should have known better."

I shook my finger at them. I was enjoying myself. Both of them looked guilty, and a bit sorry for themselves.

"Don't tell Gran, will you?" said Dad. "After all, we weren't to know Wild Thing would be raging around the house. We thought she was fast asleep— Hey! Would you look at that?"

Wild Thing *was* asleep! While we had all been talking she had curled up on Wes's sleeping bag – which had fallen to the floor – and now she was breathing deeply with her thumb in her mouth and her eyes tight shut.

She looked sweet. She always does when she's

asleep. Actually it's the *only* time she ever looks sweet.

"I guess she's had a tiring night," said Wes ruefully, rubbing his head.

Dad picked Wild Thing up and carried her up the stairs. I stayed behind. I wanted to ask Wes something.

"Wes," I said, "do you think Dad misses being in Monkey Magic?"

Wes picked the sleeping bag off the floor and began spreading it out on the couch. "I dunno, Katie. I think he likes having a chat about old times. And he does still write songs for us."

"Yes, but he doesn't do gigs or go on tour. Do you think he might ever join the band again – properly?"

"Nah – can't see it."

I flinched. "Why not? Don't you want him any more?"

My voice was suddenly all wobbly. Wes looked surprised.

"Yeah, course we'd *want* him. In fact, if you

want to know, I was trying to persuade him to play some gigs with us tonight. Not that it did any good. All I meant *was*, whenever we've tried to get him back, your dad says he isn't interested. He likes being at home with you girls. Not out on the road."

"But –" I said. "But –"

Wes yawned. "Can't see Tom changing his mind."

"I'm sure he would," I said. "I mean, who wouldn't want to be a Big Rock Star? Playing to huge crowds – and – and staying in nice hotels," I added, a bit lamely. I didn't say anything about fancy cars and swimming pools and lounging about on a sun lounger wearing shades. I didn't want Wes to think I was shallow.

"It's not that amazing, sleeping in a hotel every night," Wes said.

"What, even a fancy one, with – with room service and everything?"

"Yeah, even a fancy one. I'll tell you something, Katie, I've had more fun tonight, sleeping on your couch, than I've had in a long while. Yeah – and that includes your baby sister bashing me round the head."

I found this very hard to believe. I mean, who would want to sleep on our crummy old sofa? How much fun can that be?

But Wes was yawning his head off, and before I could argue, he said to me, "And now I'm going to sleep, if that's all the same to you. Sweet dreams!"

On my way to bed, I met Dad on the landing. He told me Wild Thing was tucked up safe in her own bedroom, and gave me a goodnight kiss.

I climbed under the duvet and was so tired I fell asleep straight away. I didn't hear any snoring, and I didn't dream about any crocodiles either!

10

Wild Thing agreed to sit down at school in the end. She wouldn't do it because *I* told her to, or Gran, or Miss Randolph, or even Mr Bartle, the head teacher. But, amazingly, after Dad had a word with her, she did.

"How did you do it?" I asked Dad.

Dad looked smug. "I am her father, after all. That counts for something. I haven't spent all these years bringing you both up, day in day out, without learning a thing or two about children."

And I hadn't spent all these years being a child, day in day out, without learning a thing or two about my dad!

"You *bribed* her," I said.

"I provided a small reward," said Dad.

"A bribe," I said. "What are you giving her?"

"A Peppy the Pop Princess DVD," Dad said, "if she sits on her bottom when her teacher tells her to."

I was shocked. "But you *hate* Peppy the Pop Princess," I said. "Peppy and her Popsters – yuck! You say it's candyfloss for the ears, and it's ruining children's ideas about music, and that it's a sign of the decline of popular culture and that—"

"OK, OK," Dad said. "I know. But I was desperate. Tell you what, Kate, I'll buy *you* something if you like."

"I am not going to be bribed to forget about a bribe," I said. "Although actually – come to think of it, I would like some new tunes for my MP3 player."

"Done!" said Dad.

After that, we actually had a couple of fairly peaceful weeks. (Or as peaceful as they can be with Wild Thing.) Summer was over, but it was still warm enough to go to the skateboard park with Zach and Bonnie. As we practised our moves, we'd spot their mum in the distance. She was wearing her tracksuit as she jogged along with Sugar and Sweet bounding after her, terrifying the squirrels.

Sometimes Wild Thing came too. She brought her little scooter and did blood-curdling jumps on the ramps, terrifying everybody! One day she crashed off a ramp and the wheel of her scooter came off. Dad wouldn't buy her another one (it was still quite new) so Wild Thing insisted that she could manage just as well with one wheel. She would be famous for her one-wheel scooter jumps, she reckoned. Soon everyone would want a one-wheel scooter, like her.

Personally, I wasn't holding my breath.

As well as creating mayhem on her scooter, Wild Thing was also still obsessed with bottoms. For example, she was keeping a list of bottom words.

Josephine Brents
Botum Words

Botum
Bum
Bee hynd
Baksid
But
Reer End

Stop talking about bottoms! – Kate

Wild Thing said Miss Randolph would be really pleased when Wild Thing took in her list of Bottom Words for Show and Tell.

I wasn't so sure.

Wild Thing continued playing the Bottom Biting Game, too. In fact, no bottom was safe any more, in our house!

Just imagine it. . .

You are quietly brushing your teeth before going to bed. You are thinking sleepy thoughts about the next day when suddenly. . .

"Owww!" you yell, clutching your behind. Yes, it's Wild Thing.

Or. . .

You are walking along the street, on your way to the skate park, wondering if Zach and Bonnie will be there waiting for you. Suddenly somebody leaps out at you from behind a lamp post.

"Eek!" you shriek. It's Wild Thing.

Or. . .

You are about to put your grubby T-shirt into the laundry to be washed. You lift up the lid of the basket and who is waiting there—

You guessed it. Wild Thing!

It was especially bad because, although I don't think she meant to, sometimes, in the heat of the moment, she really *bit*. I inspected my bum each night, convinced it would be covered in bite marks. But it was much the same as usual.

When she wasn't trying to bite me, she was

trying to get *me* to bite *her*. It's not very relaxing trying to watch TV when you've got Wild Thing prancing around wiggling her rear end. "Go on, Kate! Bite me. Try and get my bum!"

One Saturday there was a knock at the door. Gran had taken Wild Thing to her swimming class so there was only Dad and me in the house. Dad was busy mopping the floor (Wild Thing's bare feet had actually stuck to the tiles that morning and had to be peeled off, so he reckoned it was time) and he yelled over the sound of the radio, "Kate, would you get that?"

I put down my book and went to answer the door.

It was Zach.

"Oh hi," I said.

He looked a bit awkward. "Hi Kate – I was wondering, is your dad in?"

"Sure," I said. "He's just doing some mopping."

We went into the kitchen. Dad wasn't exactly mopping. Not any more. Instead he was gripping the mop like it was a guitar in one hand and slashing it with the other hand, as he yelled, "Yeah, yeah, yeah!"

Not for the first time, I wished my dad was a nice, boring dentist.

I coughed. That didn't do much good (not with all the rock music on the radio) so I yelled, "Dad!"

"Hey, guys," said Dad, coming back to earth and turning down the radio. I squelched across to the fridge to fetch Zach and me some juice.

"Sorry about that," said Dad. "I was just listening to the radio . . . and then I got a new idea for the song I'm working on. It's a great song, Kate; you're going to love it. It's the one I was playing to Wes the other night. . ."

"Wow, is it going to be a new song for Monkey Magic then?" Zach spoke in a hushed voice. He was really impressed, I could tell. "That's great! I love Monkey Magic!"

"Oh, I dunno," said Dad. "It might not be for anybody. Just me. Anyway, what are you two up to?"

Zach looked uncomfortable again. He kept shifting from foot to foot.

"Well," he said, "thing is, I'm in this band with some mates at school. And we're supposed to be playing at Parents' Assembly a few weeks from now. And we were wondering – I mean we all love Monkey Magic – and I wondered if you'd mind if we played one of your songs – you know that song you wrote, the one that goes *Wild, wild, wild. . .*" and he began to hum the chorus to Wild Thing's favourite song!

I gave a sort of groan. I couldn't stop myself.

"No problem," said Dad, grinning. "Though I don't think Kate will be too pleased, will you, Kate?"

"What do you mean?" asked Zach.

"Oh, nothing. I don't mind at all," I said quickly. After all, Zach and his band singing that song would be completely different from Wild Thing singing it.

"How come you don't play anything, Kate?" asked Zach.

Before I could say anything, Dad said, "She *does* play. Guitar and saxophone. She's good, too!"

I blushed with surprise. I never knew Dad thought I was good.

Zach said, "Hey. Why don't you play sax in our band?"

I was really taken aback. "Oh – no – I couldn't. . ."

"Course you could," said Dad. He had abandoned the mop now, and picked up his guitar, but it didn't seem to stop him butting into our conversation whenever he felt like it.

"Well, I'm not sure I want to."

"Go on, Kate," said Zach. "A sax player would be cool."

I hesitated. I like playing sax and guitar – but I like it when it's just for me. Besides, I didn't want to make a fool of myself. "No thanks," I said. I could feel my face going hot again. "Honestly. It's not my thing."

"That's funny – you seem keen on the idea of *me* playing in a band, I've noticed," said Dad. "So why not *you*?"

I glared at him. He should be sticking up for me! "That's different. . ." I began. But at that moment the door banged, and there was the sound of loud shrieks. Wild Thing was back from her swimming lesson.

The next moment she was bounding around the kitchen like a kangaroo, waving her damp swimming suit round her head.

"I saved someone's life!" she bellowed. "I'm a hero!"

"She didn't – did she?" I asked Gran, who had followed her into the kitchen.

Gran pursed her lips. "She *did* jump in—"

"It was a boy called Lewis, and I life-saved him!" Wild Thing interrupted. "Like this!" And she leapt at me and grabbed me in a headlock. She almost yanked my head off.

"Let go!" I squawked. "You're strangling me."

Wild Thing let go, and then started showing us how she had plunged to the rescue, using the kitchen table as the side of the pool. She almost landed on Zach's head.

Dad said, "What really happened?"

Gran explained. "She *did* jump in, which I suppose was quite brave of her, considering she can only swim a few strokes without armbands—"

"BRAVE!" yelled Wild Thing. "I was a brave girl in hospital! *And* at the swimming pool!"

"But," continued Gran, "the point *is*, that boy would never have been in the water in the first place if she hadn't pushed him!"

"I did not push him!"

"You most certainly did. I saw you with my own eyes."

"I only pushed him because he pushed me first."

"That may be true," Gran admitted. "He did seem a bit of a bully. But you're very lucky the instructor didn't see you. I wouldn't have blamed her if she'd refused to teach either of you again!" She sighed.

"What are you doing here?" Wild Thing asked Zach.

Before Zach could say anything, Dad said, "He came to tell us about his band. He'd like Kate to join. And I think it's a great idea."

"No," shouted Wild Thing. She stuck out her chest. "Not Kate! Only *I* get to be a Rock Star!"

She danced past, and her damp swimsuit hit me *SLAP* in the face. It was horrible, all cold and clammy. It was like being whacked with a wet fish. (Not that I've ever been whacked by a wet fish, but I'm sure that's what it feels like.)

It made me really mad, I can tell you.

And something inside of me snapped.

"Well, that's where you're wrong," I told her. "I can sing in tune – unlike some people. I can play guitar – you just pretend. And I can play saxophone. You can't. So I'd be much better in a band than you. And I'm going to. So there!"

"So you *are* playing with us?" asked Zach.

"Yes!" I said.

Almost as soon as I said it, I wondered what I'd done. What if Zach's friends didn't want me? What if they were all a million times better than me? What if I made a horrible mistake at Assembly and played lots of wrong notes, or dropped my sax on my foot and went hopping round the stage and everybody laughed?

Still, it was too late to change my mind now.

And although I was really terrified, I was really excited too, in a funny, butterflies-in-the-stomach kind of way!

11

School was going OK.

I had the feeling Miss Deng had forgotten about what happened at Big Supermarket. I almost wished now I'd been brave enough to audition for the school musical. It was *Bugsy Malone*, where everyone rushes around being gangsters and throwing cream buns, and it sounded a lot of fun. But it was too late now, and maybe I wouldn't have got a part anyway. And maybe I wouldn't even have enjoyed it if I had. It was hard, though, when Bonnie kept going on and on about *her* part, and how wonderful rehearsals were, and how fantastic Miss Deng was, until I really got sick of hearing about it!

And to my relief, because the Little Ones do so

much separately, I'd hardly noticed Wild Thing. But all that changed on Thursday afternoon.

I was about to start a maths test when it all kicked off. I was staring at the sheet of questions in front of me, but I was really thinking about band practice the day before, and wondering how it went. I hoped it had gone OK. During one song, I'd had a saxophone solo, and when I'd finished Zach and his pal Henry had gone, "Way to go!" I reckoned that meant they thought I was pretty good. But I wasn't absolutely sure.

I snapped back to reality with a start when I heard Miss Deng saying, "And write your answers neatly, please. I can't mark it right if I can't read it." I quickly read the first question: *If you have two pounds and you give 50p to charity, what percentage do you have left?* And then the fire alarm went off.

We could tell it wasn't a planned fire practice from the way Miss Deng almost fell off her chair. Also, fire practice always happens on a Friday, and it was Thursday. Miss Deng leapt up like a jack-in-the-box and began hustling us all outside. Then Bonnie said she thought she could smell burning. Miss Deng hustled us even more.

Soon the playground was full of children, all hoping to be the first one to spot the flames. Some of them said they could see an orange glow. I think that was just wishful thinking, but it got the teachers really worried.

Apart from the teachers, everyone was enjoying themselves.

Maybe somebody would be trapped in the fire!

Maybe there would be a dramatic rescue!

Maybe somebody would get burnt to a cinder, or at least a little bit scorched. (Preferably one of the dinner ladies. After all, they were always scorching our sausages, so it was only fair.)

I'm sure if anyone had *really* been hurt we'd have all felt bad, but you know how it is – sometimes it's exciting to imagine a disaster. Especially if it's instead of a maths test.

"I can definitely see smoke now," said Bonnie.

I spotted Wild Thing standing with the rest of the Little Ones. She looked, as Gran would say, "as if butter wouldn't melt in her mouth". (In case you don't know, that means all sweet and innocent. Though what that has to do with butter, I really don't know.)

It is always when Wild Thing looks the most innocent that she has been the most dreadful. But I didn't guess that *she* was to blame, until Mr Bartle the head teacher went over to the Little Ones to talk to Miss Randolph.

Soon afterwards I overheard the words "Josephine Brent" and then "responsible for all this trouble".

My heart plummeted. *Oh no*, I thought. *What has she done now?*

But it took a long, long while before I was able to work out the whole story.

This is what had happened. . .

It was just a quiet, peaceful afternoon for the Little Ones. Miss Randolph was doing some finger painting. Her helper, Ms Cooper, was supervising the sand pit, and. . .

. . .*nobody was paying attention to Wild Thing.*

Now, one of the things about Wild Thing is that she gets bored easily. You would think that sticking and gluing and painting, and playing with sand and play dough, and learning about numbers and looking at picture books would keep her busy, but—

"We'd done all that," she explained afterwards. "I wanted something new."

So what Wild Thing did was she found a load of toilet rolls in a box in the caretaker's cupboard (even though she wasn't supposed to *be* in the caretaker's cupboard, or anywhere near it) and she took those toilet rolls and she stuffed them down all four toilets in the Little Ones' cloakrooms.

She got her friend Max, who used to go to her playgroup, to help. Max was a bit unsure.

"We'll get into trouble!" he moaned. "Miss Randolph will be cross!"

(Max is a bit of a moaner.)

Wild Thing told Max that *toilet rolls* were called *toilet rolls* because they were supposed to go down *toilets*. It stood to reason, she said. It was all in the name.

"Well. . ." said Max.

"And the more the better," said Wild Thing.

So that's what they did. There were seventeen toilet rolls altogether.

They used the mop, which Wild Thing also found in the caretaker's cupboard, to help push them down.

After they had finished, Wild Thing had second thoughts. I think she actually got a bit worried about what she had done. So then she and Max tried to get the toilet rolls out again. Only they couldn't. They were wedged.

So then they tried *flushing* them down.

That was a mistake. The water couldn't go down because the pipe was blocked with toilet paper. But Wild Thing and Max didn't realize that. They flushed the toilets again.

And again.

And again.

Until the water rose up and up and overflowed all over the floor.

"It was like a lake," said Wild Thing afterwards. "It was like the sea."

What did they do next? Did they try to mop it up? Did they call for help? Did they admit what they had done?

No. They went back to join the rest of the Little Ones for Singing Time. They sat on the carpet, good as anything, and joined in with a song about Noah's Ark.

It was not long before somebody needed to go to the toilet. (You know what they are like at that age. They have to go all the time.)

It was Alfie Carruther. A moment later he was back.

"Oh! Oh!" he squeaked.

"What's the matter, Alfie?" asked Miss Randolph.

Alfie squeaked some more, and at last he managed a whole word. "Wet!"

Of course Miss Randolph got the wrong idea. She thought *Alfie* was wet. She thought he had not managed to get to the toilet in time.

"Never mind, Alfie," she cooed. "Just a little accident. We'll soon sort you out."

She led Alfie by the hand back to the toilets. When she got there, she saw at once it was not the kind of accident she was used to. Not even *all* the Little Ones could have produced a pool that size!

(Besides, it was the wrong colour.)

Miss Randolph panicked. Now, why she thought ringing the school fire alarm was a good idea, nobody will ever know. I suppose it was because there wasn't a *flood* alarm. Otherwise she would have rung that.

And that's how the whole of Pilkington Primary ended up in the playground – when they should have been doing maths or spelling instead – shrieking about flames and fire engines and generally having the best Thursday afternoon anybody could remember.

Except for me. Because by this time I knew that Wild Thing was somehow to blame.

Somebody else had worked out the same thing.

"Oh my goodness," said Bonnie loudly. "One of the Little Ones has caused a flood!"

Everyone in our class stopped yapping and turned to listen. I felt myself going red.

Bonnie looked straight at me. "It *must* be YOUR sister."

"We don't know that," I said.

"It's the worst thing any of them has ever done!"

Bonnie was hopping from one foot to the other with excitement. I was hoping nobody was listening to her.

"It's the worst thing *anyone* has ever done in the whole history of the school!"

"Please, stop it, Bonnie, can't you?"

"And just think," Bonnie went on. "She's *your* sister. She'll be famous! The worst child this school ever had."

Bonnie was really enjoying herself. To be fair, in all her excitement she probably thought I was enjoying it too. Still, if she'd stopped to think, she'd have remembered that, unlike her, and unlike Wild Thing, *I* don't like to be the centre of attention.

Then I saw Mr Bartle leading Wild Thing off. Wild Thing didn't look too worried, though. She gave me a big grin and a wave as she went by.

Luckily, none of my class were paying much attention, because an enormous red fire engine had just pulled up, with all its sirens blaring. All the kids were too busy pointing and shouting to notice Wild Thing.

But not Miss Deng. "Your sister has caused a considerable amount of damage!" she snapped, as if it were *my* fault. Then she marched off to tell everyone to calm down, it was only a fire engine.

It was so unfair. It wasn't anything to do with me. It was all down to Wild Thing!

12

Bonnie was right. Wild Thing *did* become famous. Well, not world-famous. Not hundreds-of-camera-flashes-going-off-every-time-she-stepped-out-of-the-front-door or hordes-of-fans-demanding-her-autograph famous. But famous among all the kids and parents and teachers at our school. Which meant famous in our neighbourhood. Which meant that wherever we went people stopped and pointed.

"Look!" they cried. "That's her. The Terrible Terror Josephine!"

It was awful.

She even got into the newspaper. All right, so it was only the local paper, and it was only page seven, right next to where they list all the jumble sales and church teas and meetings of the over-sixties clubs, but still. There was actually a photo of her holding a toilet roll.

Dad was really mad. He said Wild Thing was only a minor, and that it was an invasion of privacy, and a breach of Media Ethics, and that he was going to consult his lawyer.

I pointed out he didn't have a lawyer!

I *also* said that if he let Wild Thing answer the door to a journalist, and then chat for twenty minutes without ever asking who it was, *and* have her photo taken, all because he was so wrapped up in the new song he was writing, then he only had himself to blame!

"*You* could have asked," Dad said.

"I wasn't there. I was at Zach's practising with the band."

"Huh!" said Dad. "Who said you could join this band anyway?"

"You did! You thought it was a really good idea."

"Humph," said Dad.

In my opinion, Wild Thing didn't get into nearly as much trouble for the whole toilet-roll fiasco as she deserved. I mean, you would have thought Mr Bartle would have reported her to the police. Or made her go to another school. Or at least shouted at her for a bit. ("In my day we had the slipper!" said Gran.) But nothing happened.

Instead everyone said, "She's only little."

"She's only just started school."

"Anyway, it was *all an accident.*"

(An accident? How do you take seventeen toilet rolls out of a cupboard and wedge them down four toilets *by accident?*)

Bonnie said, "Isn't there a *prison* they can send her to? I mean, who knows what she'll do next!"

"Don't be stupid," I said witheringly. "You can't send little kids to prison!"

Bonnie and her big ideas!

"Why *can't* we send Wild Thing to prison, though?" I said to Dad later.

Dad laughed. "I thought you wanted to sell her."

"I do. But I don't think anybody would buy her."

"Well, nobody's going to put her in prison either. Although," Dad added, "I expect Miss Randolph would like to."

The whole thing bothered me. I mean, I was used to Wild Thing doing terrible things and getting away with it. But this time she had done terrible things and gotten away with it *and* she was in the newspaper too! I had never been in the newspaper. Dad has been in the newspaper, and on the radio, and on telly, playing his guitar. Even Gran was on the local news when she did a sponsored bike ride for charity. That only left me.

When I confided all this to Dad, he said there was nothing so great about having a picture of you in the paper, holding a toilet roll. I could see what he meant. I mean, better to be holding a Grammy Award for Best Song, or an Olympic gold medal, or an Oscar for Best Actress, or even the winning ticket in the school raffle. *Not* a toilet roll.

It still bothered me, though.

"Cheer up, Kate," said Dad. "They'll all forget about it soon. It's not like *that* many people have heard of her."

"I suppose you're right," I said. "It's not like she's *really* famous. That would be unbearable."

"And it's not going to happen," said Dad. "Believe me."

At least I was really enjoying the band. We practised in Zach's garage, and sometimes at school. There was Zach and Big Sam on guitar, Dylan on keyboards, Little Sam singing, Henry on drums, and me on the saxophone. (Little Sam isn't little, by the way – he's way taller than me – but he *is* littler than Big Sam, who is the tallest boy in our school and looms over me like a giraffe.)

I thought we sounded pretty good. But Bonnie didn't agree. She made grumpy remarks about "that horrible racket interrupting my homework". (Though it couldn't have, from the garage.) Then she started bringing us snacks – which was great at first, but she'd stick around, yakking and messing about and dropping crisps everywhere and stopping us playing. Until Zach told her to leave us alone and then she flounced off in a strop.

"Sisters!" said Zach. I knew exactly how he felt!

Later on, I was grumbling about Bonnie to Dad. To my surprise, he said, "Why don't you let her join in?"

"She doesn't want to join in," I said. "She thinks we're rubbish."

"Are you sure about that?" Dad asked. "Maybe she wants to join in but she won't admit it."

I thought about that. At first it seemed a crazy idea. But then I thought about how odd Bonnie had been acting recently. She had been quite off with me at school. And she seemed almost *pleased* when Wild Thing made all that trouble. If Bonnie were jealous of me joining the band, and feeling left out – well, it explained a lot.

The only thing was, I wasn't sure I wanted her in the band. A bit of me (maybe a mean, selfish bit) really liked being the only girl. But Bonnie *is* my best friend, so in the end I suggested to the others that we asked her to join. "She'll just mess things up," said Zach grumpily. But eventually, they agreed.

And guess what? She said yes straight away.

Unfortunately, Bonnie can't play anything, and she's not a great singer either. But, as Henry pointed out, anyone can play a tambourine. So that's what she did. It's a shame her rhythm isn't great – she kept banging her tambourine at the wrong moments. But at least we were friends again.

The Parents' Assembly was the following week. We were all really excited! Our first gig! Harris, who is Zach and Bonnie's big brother, said sarkily that he was going to call Simon Cowell and suggest he come along in case he wanted to sign us to a record deal. But we reckoned he was just jealous. Harris is in a band too, with other kids from the high school, but they've never even done a single gig!

"You *will* be able to come, won't you?" I said to Dad.

It was Saturday morning. Dad and me like a slow start on weekends, and that's what we were doing, with orange juice (me), strong coffee (Dad) and chocolate croissants (both of us). The Beatles were playing softly on the radio and sunlight was pouring in from the garden, where the birds were hopping about on the bird feeder. It would have been a perfect start to the weekend. . .

. . .If only it weren't for Wild Thing, roller-skating round the kitchen with chocolate all over her face!

As if that weren't bad enough, she was singing.

"There is nothing I can't do
When the sky is blue!
And whatever kind of weather
I am always very clever—"

"Quiet!" I shouted, but Wild Thing paid no attention.

"So *will* you come?" I said to Dad, trying to ignore her.

"Of course," said Dad at once. "Wouldn't miss it."

"It's at two o'clock on Wednesday," I said, for probably the twentieth time. "Do you know there's never been a band playing at the Parents' Assembly before? Only recorder groups and tame stuff like that. I hope – oh *shut up*, Wild Thing!"

Wild Thing paid no attention.

"...*So very, very clever!*" she bawled, and skated – *BANG!* – into the bin. It fell over with a crash, and all sorts of rubbish went bouncing across the floor.

Wild Thing just sat there amongst the potato peelings and coffee grounds, singing. She had a tea bag on her head.

"Very clever – I *don't* think," said Dad, eyeing the stream of rubbish.

But this time I couldn't see the funny side.

"I can't take this any more!" I told her. "Why can you never be quiet?"

"*Gran* says I'm a wonderful singer," said Wild Thing. "She says I've got a gift."

"You've certainly got a gift for singing *loudly*," said Dad. "I'm not sure that's the same thing."

I got up. "You don't sound wonderful – you sound like a cat being strangled," I told my sister. "Maybe, if you could hear our band play on Wednesday, then you'd know what music *should* sound like. But – thank goodness – YOU won't be there!"

"Yes I will," said Wild Thing.

"No you won't."

"Yes, I will. My class are doing Parents' Assembly too."

I could feel myself going cold all over. I looked at Dad accusingly. "She isn't, is she?"

Dad shrugged. "Not so far as I know."

"Wednesday, at two o'clock," said Wild Thing. "Miss Randolph said. It's in that letter."

"What letter?" I asked, looking at Dad.

Dad shrugged again. But he didn't meet my eye.

"You're just talking nonsense," I told her. Still, just to reassure myself, I got up and found Wild Thing's school bag. I fished out some crumb-covered play dough, the badge saying I WAS A BRAVE GIRL IN HOSPITAL and . . . a piece of paper.

It was a letter, saying that all the Little Ones would be performing at the next Parents' Assembly. "Aargh!" I yelled. "I don't want *our* Parents' Assembly to be the same as *her* Parents' Assembly!"

"Why not?" asked Dad, reading the letter. "Actually it will be quite handy. I'll be able to see you both perform at the same time."

"Yes, but she'll do something terrible! You know what she's like!"

Dad said to Wild Thing, "What are you doing in the Parents' Assembly?"

"We're doing a song," said Wild Thing proudly. "With instruments. I'm playing a triangle."

"There you are," said Dad to me. "How bad can it be? She's playing a *triangle*. What could go wrong?"

"Loads of things," I said, waving my arms around. "I mean, *most* five-year-olds couldn't do much with a triangle. But Wild Thing – she'll probably use it as a boomerang – or to gouge out somebody's eye . . . or else stick it up somebody's nose . . . or something."

But actually, I felt a bit better. Like Dad said, it was only a triangle. Surely even Wild Thing could bang away on a triangle without starting World War III.

Couldn't she?

14

On the afternoon of the Parents' Assembly, I could feel my stomach turning over. My hands were sweating. What I wanted to do more than anything else at that moment was run away!

I was sitting on the school stage between Bonnie and Zach. My saxophone was resting on my knee. Below us were rows and rows of faces. The whole *school* was sitting there, plus all the parents from Zach's year and from Wild Thing's year, who had come to see their kids perform.

The Little Ones sat opposite us on the stage. They were all sitting cross-legged, and some of them had percussion instruments. Wild Thing was in the front row, holding a triangle.

She didn't look at all nervous, I noticed. It was

just *me* that she was making nervous! I looked away quickly.

Bonnie smiled at me, and winked. I winked back. Sometimes Bonnie is a good best friend to have.

Mr Bartle stepped to the front of the stage. He beamed down upon the audience.

"How wonderful to see so many parents here today," he began, in his booming voice, "for this, one of our regular Parents' Assemblies. I know many of you have taken time off work specially, and I see that some of you have brought cameras to record the performances. I'm sure you won't be disappointed. And of course I'd like to thank all the children in the audience, who have so kindly taken time away from their maths tests and spellings to be here – ho, ho!"

He laughed loudly at his little joke. Everyone else smiled politely. Bonnie and I nudged each other and grinned.

"Today we are going to be hearing from some

of our littlest children – and from some of our oldest. Miss Randolph, I know you are proud to introduce your class."

Mr Bartle climbed heavily down from the stage and went to sit in the front row of the audience, right next to Alfie Carruther's dad – who happens to be the Chair of Governors. I could see Zach and Bonnie's mum sitting near the front (she is a governor too) and then, as I searched the rows of faces, I managed to pick out Dad. He was right in the middle of the audience, and Gran was sitting next to him. They waved and Dad did a thumbs up.

I was really pleased they were there.

Miss Randolph made a little speech, about how hard-working the Little Ones were, and how much practising they had done, and how much they enjoyed their music. During this speech, the Little Ones did a lot of wriggling and squirming – I just hoped none of them needed to go to the toilet.

Then Miss Randolph got them to come to the

front of the stage, and that took ages, with them all milling around and getting confused and going to the wrong places.

All the time, I was getting more and more nervous. I don't know why but I just felt that Wild Thing was going to do something dreadful. Even if she didn't mean to, I was sure she would start singing ten times as loud as everyone else, or picking her nose so everybody could see, or else she would drop her triangle on someone's foot and break their toe, or else . . . or else. . .

By the time they were ready to start, I was holding my breath.

We all sing together, yes we do
CLAPCLAP
(*Ting, ting* went the triangles.)
We all sing together, yes we do
CLAPCLAP
(*Ting, ting* went the triangles.)
'Cos we love to sing together, we are all friends together. . .

Wild Thing was doing fine. OK, so maybe

she was half a beat late with her triangle, but that wasn't the end of the world. And maybe her singing was a bit like a strangled cat . . . as usual . . . but amongst all the other squeaky, out-of-tune voices, she didn't sound *that* bad.

And OK, so the Little Ones weren't going to win any talent contests, but as far as I was concerned, the good news was that Wild Thing wasn't doing anything out of the ordinary. She wasn't embarrassing me in any way.

The Little Ones finished with "Stand By Me". (Even from that distance I could see Dad wincing. It's one of his favourite songs.) Then they all sat down again.

I breathed a huge sigh of relief. It was over!

I grinned at Wild Thing. I almost felt proud of her! She was scratching a scab on her knee, but stopped for a moment to wave at me.

Then it was our turn. Suddenly I didn't feel nervous any more. The worst was over and I felt like a great weight had been lifted – I was going to enjoy our gig!

Miss Deng announced that, as the teacher in charge of music, she was thrilled to introduce the first ever rock and roll band from Pilkington! We took our places on the centre of the stage. Zach grinned, said, "And a one, two, three—" and we were off!

It was brilliant! I did play a couple of wrong notes during "Shake, Rattle and Roll", probably because my fingers were a bit damp so that they slipped on the keys, and Bonnie was definitely off-rhythm with her tambourine, but it was great all the same. Even Mr Bartle was wagging his head in time to the music.

Wow, I can see why my dad loved being in a band! I thought.

And then we launched into Dad's song.

"She can fight
Yeah, and she can bite
She'll give you a fright. . ."

And that's when it happened. As Sam yelled out,

"IT'S THE WILD THING!" *something* launched itself on to the stage in front of us: a crazed, wild, cavorting, grimacing creature . . . my sister. Who else? She stomped. She waved her arms. She sang – in her horrible, strangled-cat voice.

"*Yeah, yeah, yeah!*" she yowled as she played air guitar.

"Geddoff!" I shouted, but she took no notice.

Bonnie stopped bashing her tambourine and gaped, and all the band members were staring at each other. "Keep going!" Zach hissed. "The show must go on!"

So we kept going.

Wild Thing kept going too.

In the audience, everybody was laughing.

"Josephine Brent!" I snarled as she went stomping past. "You're spoiling everything!"

"This is MY song!" said Wild Thing, and went on stomping.

Miss Randolph stood by the side of the stage, her hands fluttering. "Josephine – come here, now – I really must insist –"

Of course, Wild Thing took absolutely no notice of HER!

Then Miss Deng tried to help. She stood next to Miss Randolph. "Stop doing that and come here this minute!" she snapped.

Personally I would have come like lightning – I think most people would. Miss Deng is scary when she's angry. But Wild Thing took no notice.

We were on the last verse by now.

And suddenly, I had a horrible premonition of what Wild Thing was going to do next.

"She's wild, wild, wild!

Yeah!

Oh she's wild, wild, wild."

Wild Thing turned so that her back was to the audience, she crouched down a bit and . . . she *was* . . . she *really was* . . . she was going to moon the audience!

"Stop her!" I yelled.

I don't know if Miss Deng had come to the same conclusion. Anyway, she had obviously decided that Wild Thing needed to be stopped, because she suddenly came charging out on to the stage and headed straight for Wild Thing!

"Come here, you little rat!" she snarled.

(Afterwards everyone told me that I must have imagined this, because teachers are not allowed to call children rats. But I know what I heard. What's more, I don't blame Miss Deng one bit!)

Maybe Wild Thing had decided not to moon after all – maybe she had never meant to. Instead, with one dramatic slash at her air guitar, she suddenly leapt through the air – even Jimi Hendrix, my dad said later, couldn't have done it better – and went flying off the edge of the stage!

She landed right on top of Mr Bartle.

"Oooof!" said Mr Bartle – not surprising, really, as all the air had been knocked out of him by a five-year-old landing on his stomach.

I groaned. I just could not believe it.

15

Back at home, I really lost my temper with Wild Thing.

"You spoil everything!" I raged at her. "Everything!"

"But Kate," said Wild Thing, very slowly and patiently, as if I were the one that was being unreasonable, "it's MY song."

"It is *not* your song!" I snapped. "Dad did not write that song for you. And just because you think he did, it gives you no right to embarrass me in front of the whole school!"

"I don't think she meant—" began Dad.

"I've had enough!" I shouted. "I can't even set foot in school without everyone saying '*You're Josephine's sister, isn't she dreadful, can't you do anything about her?*' The only good thing that's happened to me this term was being in the band! And now she's spoiled that, too!" A great tidal wave of tears came rushing up into my eyes and nose. I raced out of the room and into the bathroom and locked the door. I didn't come out until I'd scrubbed away the tears.

Of course, they tried to talk me round. Gran and Dad got Wild Thing to make me a card to apologize. It had "Sorry!" and "Lurv you!" and "Plees forgiv me!" scrawled all over it in golden glitter pen, and red love hearts glued on, and a picture of Wild Thing weeping enormous teardrops into a giant hanky. But I wasn't about to forgive her. No way! Not *ever*.

At bedtime, she crept into my room, wearing her blue dressing gown and an angelic expression. She put a pink flower on my pillow.

I just turned my head away.

The next day, Wild Thing gave me a gigantic chocolate teddy bear that she'd bought from the fancy deli on the corner. I guess it was Dad's idea, but she *did* use all the money in her piggy bank.

I was going to turn it down . . . really, I was. But it seemed a shame to waste it. So I munched a tiny bit of the bear's left paw. Mmmm! It was the creamiest, sweetest chocolate I had ever tasted! Maybe I could forgive Wild Thing after all. . .

That's when Zach and Bonnie came round.

"Have you seen it?" gasped Bonnie. "Have you?"

"Have I seen what?" I asked, puzzled.

Zach went all dramatic. "Take me to your laptop!" he said.

Dad and I gathered round curiously as Zach opened the lid.

Zach typed in "Wild Thing" – and suddenly there, on the screen, was my sister. Screeching. Jumping. Strumming away on her horrible air guitar. And then, as Miss Deng tried to grab her, leaping right on top of poor Mr Bartle!

It seemed one of the parents at the assembly had videoed the whole thing. And then put it on YouTube. After that, as Zach said, it had gone "viral".

I wasn't sure what this meant at first, so Zach explained that millions of people had seen it. As if Wild Thing was a really nasty flu, and the whole world had caught it.

I was in the video too. You could just about make out my shocked face in the background as my sister went cavorting around the stage like something that had escaped from a zoo. But that didn't make me feel any better.

"I can't believe it," I kept saying to Dad.

"Don't worry," said Dad. "I'll get on to Mr Bartle. That parent had no business posting that video without permission. I'll get it taken down."

"A bit late," I pointed out, "when the whole world has seen it!"

Wild Thing, of course, thought it was just great that she was on the internet. Whatever anybody else said, Wild Thing got the idea she had been really clever.

"And now the World-famous Wild Thing is having her breakfast," she would say.

"The World-famous Wild Thing is watching TV."

"The World-famous Wild Thing is eating her fish fingers with tomato ketchup *and* mayonnaise."

It was enough to make you choke on a chip!

Mr Bartle did get the film taken down, but that wasn't the end of it. About a week later, Dad got a phone call. I was doing my homework at the time, but I could hear part of Dad's conversation in the background.

"Hey, Wes," he said. "How're you doing?"

"Oh yeah, you saw it. . . Yeah, it made a lot of people laugh. . . What's that? Really?. . . Really?. . . *Really?*. . . Yeah, man, great to talk to you too."

And Dad hung up.

I stopped reading and said, "What did Wes want?"

"Oh, not much," said Dad. I thought he looked a bit peculiar.

"He must have wanted *something*. You sounded really surprised."

"Oh. Well. Seems like Monkey Magic have been asked to play that song – you know – Wild Thing's song – at a big awards ceremony on TV in a couple of weeks' time."

"Wow!" I said.

"And – you know the new song I wrote recently? Well, I finished it and sent it to Wes, and they all like it and . . . well, they're going to record it and they're going to play it at the awards ceremony too."

"That's amazing!" I said.

"And they've asked me to play guitar with them. At the awards ceremony."

"Wow," I said. "So you'll be on TV?"

"I guess so."

"Then . . . then you're practically back in the band. You're going to be a big, famous rock star after all!"

All kinds of ideas were rushing through my head. Like: *Fantastic, Dad's going to be famous!*

Maybe we'll be rich! Maybe we'll move to London! Maybe we'll move to Hollywood! Maybe I'll get to hang out by swimming pools after all! But another bit of me was feeling – well – a little bit scared, I guess. And I wasn't even sure why.

It all came out in a garbled rush of questions. "Are you going on tour? How about their next album? Will you be on posters? Will everyone recognize you? Will they want your autograph? Will you need bodyguards?"

Dad said, "Enough questions! Calm down a moment. You're making my head spin."

I calmed down. But Dad looked at me so seriously that I began to feel nervous.

"What do you think would happen if I went away on tour? And left you two girls behind?"

"Well . . . Wild Thing and I would probably kill each other. . ."

"Exactly."

"But don't let that stop you!" I urged him. "We don't mind! Even if we are – uh – dead."

"Kate," said Dad, "come here a moment."

I went over and Dad put his arm round me. I leaned against him.

"Listen to me, Kate. I may play at this awards ceremony. I certainly plan to write more songs. But I am *not* going out tour, and I'm not going to rejoin Monkey Magic – not full time, anyway. I'm never going to be a Big Rock Star.  So get that idea right out of your head. I'm going to stay right here and look after you two girls. Maybe if your mum was alive it would be different ... but there's only me, and I'm going to do the very best job I can!"

"Oh," I said in a small voice. I couldn't work out if I was disappointed or relieved. And – something was really bothering me. "But – but then is it *our* fault?" I blurted out. "I mean, if it's just *us* that's stopping you – looking after us, Wild Thing and me – then, well, aren't you really disappointed?"

"No," said Dad, hugging me. "I love music, and that's why I do what I do – it's not because I want to be a famous rock star. As long as I can play my guitar – and as long as we all have enough to get by – that's good enough for me."

"Then it's good enough for me, too!" I said, giving him a huge hug back. It was true. At that moment, anyway, I didn't give a monkey's (no, not even a magic one) for all the luxury hotels, and swimming pools, and purple limos, and celebrity parties in the world. You could chuck them in a gigantic great bin for all I cared!

Dad had a big grin on his face. He couldn't grin like that if he were feeling sad about giving up a life of fame and fortune.

"There's only one thing I really want," Dad told me. "To bring up you girls and see you grow into decent human beings."

"Good luck with that," I said. "'Cos you've got your work cut out for you with Wild Thing."

Dad chuckled. "You can say that again. But I'm not giving up!"

So that was that.

I went to put my homework upstairs, and as I went I found I was whistling. Dad *wasn't* unhappy. We weren't stopping him from following his dream. We weren't ruining his life. And we still had his TV appearance to look forward to. I mean, just wait until I told Zach that Dad was playing at the big awards ceremony!

When I got to the landing I stopped whistling. I tiptoed past Wild Thing's door, the way I've done ever since she started her Bottom Biting Game. Just in case she comes out and bites me! But there was no danger.

She was screeching away inside, pretending to be a rock star, just as she's done every single day since she saw herself on YouTube. She was making too much noise to hear me.

I may not have a famous dad, but I've certainly got an *infamous* sister! (Which means famous too – only in a *bad* way.)

Just my luck!

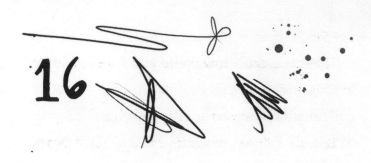

16

On Friday afternoon, when the bell rang, Miss Deng called me over for a word. She hadn't said much to me about the whole Wild Thing Assembly Disaster, so I felt a bit nervous as I waited to find out what she wanted.

"Your sister made quite a display of herself the other day," she said. "*And* all over the internet too."

"I know," I said. "We try, but there's nothing we can do with her."

Miss Deng smiled. Then she said, "I hadn't realized until then that you came from a musical family."

"Well, *Dad's* musical. I wouldn't say the same for Wild – I mean, my sister."

"And *you're* musical too, Kate, or you wouldn't play the saxophone. Can you sing?"

"Er. . ."

"I bet you can. How come you didn't audition for *Bugsy Malone?*"

The honest answer to this was:

Because I Know You Hate Me and You'd Never, Ever Give Me a Part

or

Because I'm Shy and So I Talk Myself Out of Things Even If Secretly I Want to Do Them.

But you can't give teachers honest answers, can you? Especially teachers as scary as Miss Deng. So I just went *Er* and *Um* and *I don't know*.

Only then Miss Deng asked me to sing. Right there and then. And because she is so scary, I didn't even try to argue. I thought I sang OK. In tune, anyway. And I must have because – she gave me a part! In *Bugsy Malone*! Not a big part, because those have all been cast. But still. . .

I'm in the school musical! Hooray!

But do you know what Wild Thing said about it when she heard?

"All because of me," she said, banging her chest like she was Tarzan or something.

"What do you mean?" I asked.

"She means, Miss Deng only realized *you* might be a good singer after she saw Josephine singing at the Parents' Assembly," said Gran.

"What!" I shrieked. "It was nothing to do with it! It was all because of my saxophone playing! Anyway, Wild Thing sounded like a cat being strangled! *Nobody* would think I might be a good singer because of her!"

Gran shrugged. "I've heard a lot worse from some of your dad's friends. And they even get paid for it!"

"I don't owe Wild Thing anything!" I said. "All she's ever done is ruin my life."

"OK," said Dad. "But try not to fall out with her while your gran's in charge."

Dad was going down to London for the weekend and he wouldn't be back until Sunday evening. He was going to play in the Big Awards Ceremony with Monkey Magic. They were going to sing Dad's new song, and also the Wild Thing song. It was all going to be on TV – but we wouldn't be able to watch it until a few nights later. It was going to be recorded.

Dad had explained that the TV stations don't show the awards live, in case anybody does anything they shouldn't do. Apparently there are lots of crazy people like Wild Thing in the music industry, and the TV people like to edit them out if they don't behave. (I wish I could edit Wild Thing out.)

While Dad was away, I planned to ignore Wild Thing. It wasn't too difficult, as it turned out. Gran let me invite Bonnie over for a sleepover on Saturday, and while we were playing computer games, or painting our toenails funny colours, or pretending to tell each other's fortunes, Gran did baking and crafts with Wild Thing. I think some glue might have got into the cake mix, judging by the taste, but it was worth eating gluey cupcakes to have a little peace and quiet!

On Sunday, I was determined to wait up to

see Dad and hear all about the awards ceremony. But he phoned to say his train was delayed, and Gran said I had to go to bed. I must have been really tired after the sleepover, because even though I meant to stay awake, I fell asleep almost at once. I think I half woke when Dad got in. I'm almost sure I heard Dad and Gran say goodnight, and then the front door closing as Gran went home. But then I fell straight back to sleep.

I don't know how much later it was when I woke again, but it was pitch black. What woke me was a horrible coldness on my back. It was as if somebody had got a bag of frozen peas out of the freezer and stuck them down my pyjamas. Then a voice said in my ear, "Kate, are you awake?"

"I am *now*," I growled. "Now you've woken me."

"It's me, Josephine."

"I know *that*! I know!"

I gave a kind of groan. Just as soon as I was awake enough, I was going to turn round and thump her, or maybe smother her with pillows.

"I can't sleep. You see," Wild Thing explained

in a loud whisper, *"there's a monster in the house."*

I ground my teeth. I really did. I couldn't believe that she had done this to me *again*.

"For the very last time," I hissed at her, "THERE IS NO MONSTER."

"There is. I heard it. I saw it too."

"Where?"

"Just now. On the landing."

"It was Dad, going to the bathroom."

"It wasn't. It really wasn't, Kate."

I'd had enough of her craziness. I tried to shove her out of bed with my foot. Only she's heavier than you'd think and she didn't budge. "Wild Thing, if you don't get out of my bed this minute. . ."

I stopped. Because at that moment I heard a noise.

"It's just Dad," I said. "I'll prove it to you."

I threw back the covers and leapt out of bed. There was no way I was going to be frightened by imaginary monsters this time!

"Don't go, Kate!" Wild Thing quavered.

"You stay there, scaredy-cat," I said. I went across the landing and peered into Dad's bedroom.

It was empty.

The bathroom was empty too.

I frowned. That was strange. Then again, Dad often sits up watching TV, especially if he's been out late. He'd probably just fallen asleep on the sofa.

I started for the stairs. I thought I might as well check.

I could hear a little squeaking noise as I went back across the landing. It was Wild Thing, peeping round the door of my bedroom. "Kate! Don't go!"

She really must have thought there was a monster out there. Nothing else usually scares her. The silly little coot!

But not me. Not this time.

I had only gone a little way down the stairs when I heard a noise. It was as if somebody was moving around – but quietly, so as not to disturb anyone. It came from the direction of the kitchen.

For a moment I felt quite scared. But then I realized. It must be Dad. He was probably fixing himself a hot drink.

I thought I might as well say hello. Now that I was up.

I started off down the stairs again. But near the bottom, something stopped me in my tracks.

The door to the living room was open. And through the doorway I could see Dad, fast asleep on the sofa.

But if Dad was fast asleep, who was it moving about in the kitchen?

It was then I noticed that the front door was slightly open. Dad had probably forgotten to lock it when Gran left. But it wouldn't be standing open . . . *unless somebody had crept in.*

At that moment I really did feel sick. My hands felt cold. And my stomach felt as if somebody was squeezing it. Hard.

And then the kitchen door opened.

It wasn't a monster. It wasn't Gran either. And

it wasn't one of Dad's friends, stopping by for a drink.

It wasn't anyone I recognized.

It was a man in a grey tracksuit. The hall was dim so I couldn't see him very well. But there was something about him I didn't like. It was the shifty way he kept glancing around him. He looked mean. And big. He was carrying a bin bag in one hand.

A burglar.

I almost screamed. But I was afraid that if Dad came running – especially if he was half-asleep and not really sure what was going on – then the burglar would hit him. And he's not very tough, my dad, to be honest with you. He always says he's a bit of an old softy.

Besides, the burglar was lots bigger than him.

So I just sat and watched, terrified to move, as the burglar started rummaging in our dresser. Looking for money, I reckoned. Luckily he didn't see me, crouched in the shadows on the stairs.

I suppose I might have just sat there and watched the burglar escape. In a way it would have been the sensible thing to do. Only then I saw something that changed everything.

The burglar was holding my mum's picture. The one in a silver frame that my dad loves so much.

Suddenly I felt really mad. The burglar had no business taking Mum's picture! No business at all! Dad had been upset enough that time

Wild Thing almost got ketchup on it. He'd be miserable if he lost it for ever.

So when the burglar stopped rummaging and made for the front door, instead of just watching him go, I stuck out my foot.

And the burglar tripped right over it.

He fell on to the floor with a clatter. For a second he just lay there. Then he began to get up.

That's when I got really scared.

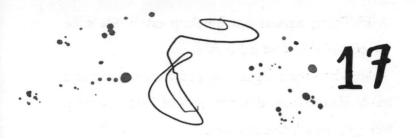

17

I bawled, "Daaaaaaaaad!"

The burglar was still getting up. I don't know what he planned to do next. I didn't *want* to know. I was desperately trying to remember some karate moves that Dad's friend Bill once showed me, but my mind went blank. Anyway, before I could move a muscle, *something* came flying past me. A little ball of hissing, snarling rage.

It was Wild Thing.

She didn't have her armour on, or her battle mace, but she was formidable all the same.

The burglar gasped as Wild Thing crashed into him. He stumbled, tripped over the rug and fell on to the floor. He was trying to get up again – but then he yelled really, really loudly.

"OWWWWW!"

She had. Yes – she really had. You've guessed it. Wild Thing had bitten him on the bum.

The burglar yelled some more. I guess she bit him really hard. Then he tried to kick Wild Thing, but she dodged.

"You leave her alone!" I yelled.

"You leave me alone!" yelled Wild Thing.

"You leave my kids alone!" yelled Dad, shooting out of the living room.

The burglar was on his feet by now, so Dad tried to rugby-tackle him. In case you don't know, that means a flying leap where you grab someone's legs and bring them down to the ground. But it didn't work very well. Perhaps because Dad has never played rugby.

Instead of the burglar, it was *Dad* who ended up on the floor. Wild Thing and me were both trying to get at the burglar (I think we had gone a bit crazy) but we got all tangled up with each other and Dad. The burglar went racing out of the house and was gone.

He had dropped his bag of loot. Mum's

photo had fallen on to the rug. I picked it up and hugged it.

Dad ran for the phone. First he called the police, and then he called Bonnie's mum. I thought it was a bit much, phoning Bonnie's mum at half three in the morning and expecting her to catch our burglar. But it was a good idea really. You see, all Bonnie's mum did was she watched from her window until she saw the burglar running past, and then she opened her front door, and her two enormous dogs, Sugar and Sweet, galloped out. They went racing after the burglar while Bonnie's mum yelled, "Go get 'em, girls!"

And they did. When the police arrived, sirens blaring, they found our burglar with Sugar and Sweet sitting on top of him.

They took the burglar away, but one of the policemen came round to ask us what had happened, and Bonnie's mum came too. Dad fixed teas and hot chocolates and we all sat round the kitchen table.

The policeman turned out to be PC Blunt – the same policeman who had come when Wild Thing had stuck the plastic guitar up her nose. He reminded us that he'd told us then there were a lot of break-ins. *And* he'd told us to be careful to lock our front doors too – as I reminded Dad!

"I thought I *had* been careful," said Dad, looking sheepish.

"You silly poop!" said Wild Thing to Dad. And she was right!

Bonnie's mum was very pleased that it was her dogs that had caught the burglar. She and PC Blunt stayed for ages, talking about crime and dog-handling, but eventually Dad said he really needed to get Wild Thing and me off to bed. So they left.

After they had gone, Dad picked up Mum's photo and gazed at it for a long while. Then he turned to look at us.

"I have two very brave girls," he told us. And he gave us a huge hug.

So now we are famous again. Only this time it's not just Wild Thing. It's me too. (And Sugar and Sweet, of course.)

We all got our photos in the newspaper, on the front page this time. We were on TV too. The news reports used words like "brave", "courageous" and "quick-witted". It made me blush. Especially when I read the bit about how it was *me* who tripped up the burglar.

At school, Mr Bartle had a Special Assembly all about Wild Thing and me. He said we were "brave", "courageous" and "quick-witted" too. (He also said that nobody else should ever try to tackle a burglar the way we did, because they might get hurt, and it was far more sensible to call the police, but nobody paid much attention to that bit. They were too busy clapping and cheering.) And PC Blunt was there and he gave us two enormous certificates, with FOR BRAVERY written on them in gold letters.

When we showed him our certificates, Dad said he was very proud of us. He said Mum would have been proud too. He also said the last thing he would have expected was that Wild Thing would ever get a certificate for biting somebody. Especially on the bum.

Gran agreed. She said It Just Goes To Show That You Never Can Tell.

She is right. Especially when it comes to Wild Thing.

With Wild Thing, You Never Can Tell.

And for once I am not too upset with my sister. I am not daydreaming about selling her – not this week, anyway. I am enjoying the fame and the glory instead. I reckon it's loads better than being the daughter of a Famous Rock Star – after all, this is something me and Wild Thing did for ourselves.

Of course, I know my sister. I suppose soon she will be famous again for doing something terrible. But until then, it's nice to have her famous for something good. And every time I think of her biting that burglar on the bottom, I have to smile.

"I told you Biting Bottoms was a good game," said Wild Thing, hanging her Certificate For Bravery upside down on the fridge.

"You are a real pain in the bum," I told her. "But once in a while, that comes in useful."

It's true. Everybody has their moment.

And whatever else you might say about her, there's nobody else like WILD THING!

Look out for Wild Thing's
next escapade
COMING SOON!

Wild THING AND Hound Dog

It was just an ordinary Thursday.

I was doing my homework at the kitchen table, Dad was searching the fridge for something for tea, and my little sister Wild Thing was under the table "cooking" something in her toy kitchen. She makes all kinds of horrible things in it, but so far nobody's ever has to eat any of it, thank goodness, because all the food is plastic. (Mind you, I think Wild Thing has tried, because some of the hot dogs and cupcakes have teeth marks.)

"I was sure we had some leftover rice. . ." Dad muttered. "And some tomatoes."

"Stir it round, stir it round!" chortled Wild Thing. She was bent over her mixing bowl with her long hair dangling down and an evil expression on her face, like a witch stirring its cauldron.

"We even seem to have run out of tuna," said Dad, peering into the cupboard. "I was sure there was one more tin."

"Don't want tuna," said Wild Thing, and she cackled an evil cackle.

"There aren't any baked beans, either."

Wild Thing cackled again and suddenly I got suspicious.

"Wait a minute. What have you got in that bowl?"

Wild Thing said nothing.

"The tuna's in there, isn't it? And the rice?"

Wild Thing still said nothing, but put her arms protectively round the mixing bowl.

"Josephine!" said Dad in his special stern voice. Josephine is Wild Thing's real name.

"It's for my lovely stew!" shouted Wild Thing. "Nobody said I couldn't!"

("Nobody said I couldn't" is one of my sister's favourite defences whenever she's in trouble.

"Nobody said I couldn't cut Kate's homework into a hundred pieces."

"Nobody said I couldn't glue a napkin to my nose."

"Nobody said I couldn't pour tomato ketchup over my head when I'm playing vampires."

"Nobody said I couldn't pretend Dad's guitar case was a canoe and paddle it down the stairs.")

"I'm glad your stew is so lovely," said Dad sternly, "because that's what YOU are going to have for dinner!"

"No!" squawked Wild Thing. "Won't!"

But for once, Dad seemed cross enough to make her do it. I watched, fascinated, as he got a big spoon out of the kitchen drawer and marched over to her mixing bowl. Then he spooned up a dollop and held it out to Wild Thing, while my sister put her hand over her mouth, screeching as loud as she could.

"Here. You made it so you can eat it—" Dad stopped short suddenly, staring at the gloopy mixture on the spoon. "Wait. Why is this stuff green?"

He was right. The lumps of tuna and rice and baked beans (and I thought I could spot pineapple chunks too) were all floating around in a bright green gloop.

"What's she put in there?" I wondered. "Frozen spinach? Lime cordial? Mint ice cream?"

"Not telling," said Wild Thing.

My dad dipped a finger into the mixture, then stuck it into his mouth. He almost fell over. "Yeurrrgh! That's disgusting!"

It was at that moment that I spotted the empty plastic bottle on the floor. "Pine Fresh Washing-up Liquid," I read aloud. "She's used the whole bottle."

However cross he was, Dad wasn't about to feed Wild Thing washing-up-liquid stew. "That still leaves the question of what we have for dinner," he said, as he dumped her mixing bowl in the sink.

"Takeaway?" I suggested hopefully.

"We did that yesterday. We can't keep doing it!"

"Lucky Dip!" cried Wild Thing.

We all looked at each other. Dad hesitated. I was sure he was going to be all sensible and say no.

"Oh, go on then," he said.

We all went into the back hall, where we keep the washing machine, the hiking boots, the sled and lots of things that we don't use that often. It's also where we keep our freezer, which is one of those big old-fashioned freezers, like a huge trunk you open from the top.

"It's a bit empty," I said, peering in. "Most of the stuff's right at the bottom."

Dad was tying a scarf over my sister's eyes. He stepped back and looked at her. "Are you sure about this?"

"Want to do Lucky Dip!" Wild Thing howled.

So Dad grabbed Wild Thing's middle. Then he dangled her over the freezer by her ankles.

Or rather, that's what he tried to do. I guess she'd been growing lately. Or maybe it was because all the food was at the very bottom of the freezer. Anyway, there was a lot of heaving and shouting from Wild Thing, while Dad tried to hold her upside down by one leg, and I helpfully grabbed hold of the other.

"Keep hold. . ."

"I am keeping hold. . ."

"Stop wriggling, Wild Thing!"

"But I can't reach!" Wild Thing screeched. She wriggled harder, trying to grab the packets of frozen food, and Dad pulled, and I pushed, and then – CRASH! – suddenly Wild Thing went slipping out of our grasp, right into the freezer. We were all so surprised that for a moment we didn't say anything. Dad and me just gasped like a pair of goldfish, while Wild Thing sat at the bottom of the freezer with oven chips in her hair.

Then we all began to laugh.

Suddenly there was a cough from behind us. Gran was standing in the doorway.

"Is there some reason why have you put poor Josephine in the freezer?" she asked. Her voice was as icy as the chips.

Even when Gran understood Lucky Dip, she didn't approve. We were back in the kitchen, and

Gran was standing in the middle of the floor, hands on hips, glaring.

"So let me get this straight. When you couldn't decide what to cook, you used to take Josephine, blindfold her, bob her into the freezer and whatever she pulled out, that was what you ate?"

"Got it in one," said Dad, a bit defiantly.

"Wild Thing got the idea from the Lucky Dip at the school fair," I said.

Wild Thing wasn't paying attention. She was too busy winding her hair round the frozen chips, as if they were curlers. Then she experimentally moved one chip towards her nostril – until Gran barked, "Josephine!" and she quickly dropped it again.

Gran turned back to Dad.

"So what happened if she pulled out lollies and chicken stock? Is that what you'd eat?"

"That's what we'd eat."

"That's the whole point," I explained. "You never knew what you'd get."

"It was fun!" Wild Thing agreed.

Gran tutted. "It's not what I'd call a balanced meal."

I love Gran. But there's no doubt she can be a bit of an old granpuss sometimes. We've had some great meals from Lucky Dip. Pizza with chocolate sauce. Potato waffles with ice cubes. Strawberries with hot dogs. OK, they may not sound great to you. But we always ate them. And enjoyed them. Sort of.

Of course Gran didn't see it that way. Still, once she had stopped tutting, she helped Dad make a really nice meal, much nicer than if we'd had Lucky Dip. Gran managed to find some eggs Dad had overlooked, and turned them into an omelette. We had peas from the freezer, as well as potato wedges, and lashings of tomato ketchup. While we were eating, the doorbell rang.

It was Wes, the lead singer in Dad's old rock band, Monkey Magic. Dad doesn't play with them much any more. But he's still good friends with them, and he often writes songs for them too.

Gran doesn't really approve of Monkey Magic (or rock music) but she does have a bit of a soft spot for Wes. He always remembers to ask how her tango classes are going. And he always praises her cooking. "This omelette is magnificent – I've eaten omelettes all over the world but you can't beat this!"

Gran preened a bit. Then she said she had to get home, because she had a big work meeting the next day. Wes told her he wouldn't see her for a while, because the band was off to the USA.

"New York, Austin, Denver, San Francisco," said Wes dreamily. "Our first big American tour!"

Wild Thing and I thought it sounded really exciting. So after Gran left, we followed Dad and Wes into the living room, and while they sat about strumming their guitars, we asked Wes questions about the tour.

"Yeah – it's going to be great," Wes said. "Hey, you should come with us, man," he said suddenly to Dad. "Back on the road again! You know you want to."

Dad shook his head.

"But you should be there, Tom. After all, you wrote half the songs."

"My touring days are over," said Dad, trying out a new riff.

"Why, man?"

"You know why. Because of the girls."

"Bring them along!" said Wes, waving a hand at Wild Thing and me, and nearly knocking over his coffee.

Wild Thing and me looked at each other.

"Yeah, we'll come too!" Wild Thing urged.

"I'd love to go to America!" I said.

"There's that small thing called School," said Dad.

"They can miss it," said Wes.

"Yeah, we can miss it," Wild Thing said. I nodded. Five weeks off school to go touring the US of A with Monkey Magic? You bet I wanted to go!

"Absolutely not," said Dad firmly. "The girls need to go to school. Their education is important. Besides," he added to Wes, "you've got Chris now. You don't need two guitarists."

Wes gave a big sigh. Wild Thing and I sighed too. For a moment we had dreamed that we might really get to go. But we should have known Dad would never let us.

Ever since our mum died, it's up to Dad to bring us up, and he takes his responsibilities seriously. He says family life and playing in a rock band don't mix. He still plays the guitar, but he spends most of his time teaching or song-writing, or working in his studio. He never goes on tour any more, even though we'd love to go with him. I can just imagine it now – sitting in the tour bus and watching the scenery roll by, waving to the fans, sitting backstage playing computer games, eating loads of junk food or else ordering room service in a fancy hotel. Dad says it isn't as much fun as it sounds – but how do we know, if he won't even let us try?

And this time it was America!

"Disneyland," I murmured. "The Grand Canyon. Hollywood."

"Zebras," said Wild Thing. "Antelopes."

I guess Wild Thing was a bit confused with her geography (after all, she is only five) because I don't think zebras and antelopes live in the USA.

I didn't say anything though. I wasn't a hundred per cent sure myself.

Wes played a few melancholy chords on his guitar. Then he said, "Hey, Tom, if you're sure you can't come, how about you and the girls look after Hound Dog for me? You'd like that, wouldn't you, girls?"

"Who's Hound Dog?" I asked.

"You never met Hound Dog? I got him from the Dog's Home. His real name's Elvis. But you see, he ain't nothing but a Hound Dog. So that's what I call him." He and Dad shared a chuckle.

Wild Thing and I looked at each other, then looked at Dad.

"Perlease, perlease, can we look after Hound Dog!" I begged.

"Yeah – want a doggy!" shrieked Wild Thing.

"Absolutely not," said Dad. "I've got a rule – two beasties are enough."

"But Goldilocks and Bug-Eyed Monster are dead," I pointed out. (Goldilocks and Bug-Eyed Monster were our goldfish.)

"I'm not talking about pets," said Dad.

It took me a moment to work out what he meant. Then: "We're not beasties!" I yelled. "C'mon, Wild Thing!"

We both flung ourselves on Dad, bashing him with cushions and jumping on him. I don't think Wild Thing had even worked out why I was cross, but she loves a rumpus, so she didn't care. As for Wes, he grabbed Dad's guitar, so it wouldn't get broken, then sat there laughing.

Dad won, eventually. He fought us off, then wrapped us up in the rug.

"The answer's still no," he panted.

"Come on, your girls are dying to have him," coaxed Wes.

"Sure they are! For five minutes. But who will end up walking him and feeding him, and scraping his poo off the pavement?" asked Dad. "Me! That's who." He pointed at me and Wild Thing. "I had years cleaning up THEIR poo when they were tiny and now I'm enjoying the rest!"

And however much we begged and pleaded – "I LOVE picking up poo!" said Wild Thing – he wouldn't budge.

Emma Barnes

has always been a bookworm. She was born and raised in Edinburgh, where she spent hours making up stories for her younger sister. Emma's first writing success came when she won a short story competition – the prize was a pair of shoes. Emma wears the shoes for school visits, where she loves to spark children's imaginations and create a passion for writing and stories. Emma now lives in Yorkshire with her husband, daughter and Rocky the dog.

www.EmmaBarnes.info